THE NANCY DREW FILES™ CASE 21

Recipe for Murder

Carolyn Keene

AN ARCHWAY PAPERBACK
Published by POCKET BOOKS
New York London Toronto Sydney Tokyo

AN ARCHWAY PAPERBACK *Original*

An Archway Paperback published by
POCKET BOOKS, a division of Simon & Schuster, Inc.
1230 Avenue of the Americas, New York, N.Y. 10020

Produced by Mega-Books of New York, Inc.

ISBN: 0-671-64227-8

First Archway Paperback Printing March 1988

10 9 8 7 6 5 4 3 2 1

Printed in the U.S.A.

IL 7+

FROM THE NANCY DREW FILES

THE CASE: Find out who killed Chef Trent Richards of the Claude DuPres International Cooking School—and why.

CONTACT: When Ned bets Nancy he can learn to outcook her, they both enroll in a school for chefs—and stir up an international plot.

SUSPECTS: Chef Claude DuPres—*the head of the school is in financial hot water.*

Chef Paul Slesak—*the highly strung gourmet thinks everyone is out to steal his recipes.*

Chef Jacques Bonet—*the handsome young Frenchman is determined to cook something up with Nancy.*

COMPLICATIONS: Claude DuPres collapses—could he have been poisoned? Chef Slesak's recipes contain some unusual ingredients. And Bonet's extracurricular interest in Nancy is bringing Ned's temper to a boil.

Books in THE NANCY DREW FILES™ Series

RECIPE FOR
MURDER

Chapter One

"Ahhh—" Nancy Drew sniffed appreciatively. The scent of barbecued chicken wafted into the air, making her mouth water.

Ned grinned. "Didn't I say I could cook?"

"You said it," Rick Williamson, one of their friends, answered for her. "We just didn't believe it."

"We still don't." Bess Marvin heaved a huge sigh and wiped her forehead. "Soon the food won't be the only thing that's cooked!"

"It should start to cool off before long," Nancy

said. The hot July sun still prickled her scalp, but there weren't many hours of daylight left. "By that time dinner might even be on the table."

"Did somebody mention food?" a girl's voice called from the other side of the Drew backyard. Slim, athletic George Fayne was bent over a croquet mallet, her eye on the red ball about a yard from hers. With a short swing she knocked her ball into her opponent's. "Aha! You're out of the yard, Ken."

Ken Hampton, another River Heights High graduate, looked at the sky. "Why me?" he asked as George placed her croquet ball next to his. She rested her foot on her blue ball, gave it a sharp crack with the mallet, and sent Ken's ball spinning across the yard to slam into the fence on the far side.

"It's too hot to play croquet," Bess observed. "All I want to do is eat."

"That's all you ever want to do," George called as she lined up her next shot.

"And all *you* ever do is compete," Bess complained to her. She glanced across the table at Nancy. "How many games has George played today? And this is after giving tennis lessons all morning! It's not human."

"At least she's busy," Nancy said with a sigh. "This summer seems to be dragging on forever."

"No new mysteries, huh?" Bess asked.

"Not a one." Pushing strands of reddish blond

hair out of her face, Nancy said, "Come on in the kitchen and help me see about the rest of the stuff."

As they headed inside, Nancy heard the hollow sound of George's croquet ball connecting with the final stake. "Okay, Hampton," George crowed with triumph, "that's three. Think you're up for another?"

"No way," Ken answered. "The next time we play a game, I get to choose."

Nancy chuckled as she cracked open the oven door. She checked on the baked beans. They were bubbling gently. A couple more minutes and they'd be ready to serve with Ned's chicken.

"Refills!" Nancy called as she carried out another pitcher of lemonade.

"Great!" Ned tossed off Nancy's father's barbecue apron and sank down beside her on the picnic bench. "This cooking takes a lot out of a guy."

"You were the one who wanted to do it," Nancy reminded him, pouring him a glass.

"I know." Ned took a huge swallow. "But believe me, this'll be the best chicken you've ever tasted. An old family recipe. It'll be worth the wait."

Nancy had just opened her mouth to answer when she suddenly smelled something burning. "The chicken!" she cried, leaping from her seat.

Smoke was billowing out the sides of the

covered barbecue. Nancy lifted the lid just as Ned reached her side. Flames were blazing around what was left of the chicken.

Quickly Ned dumped his lemonade over the ruined meat and doused the fire.

"Oh, no," he groaned, staring down at the now-blackened chicken as the others crowded around to see.

Nancy covered her mouth with her hand to hide a smile. The chicken was burned to a crisp.

"An old family recipe, huh?" Rick demanded.

"Yeah, chicken à la lemonade." George started to laugh.

"This is terrible," Nancy said, trying to sound sympathetic.

"It sure is!" Bess wailed. "Now what are we going to do? Send out for pizza?"

"Don't panic," Ned said. "We can make hamburgers or something."

"Are you kidding?" George looked appalled. "I would like to eat in this century, if you don't mind."

Everyone but Ned and Bess burst into laughter. "I can cook," Ned insisted. "I can."

"Oh, sure." Ken Hampton was laughing so hard he could barely catch his breath. "Nickerson, you couldn't cook even if you went to cooking school."

"Ned," Nancy said, "I think Ken has a good idea." Her blue eyes danced with merriment. "You've got the rest of the summer. Why not go to cooking school? I dare you. And I'll even tag along to make sure you don't burn down the school."

Ned sent her a mock glare. "Is this a challenge?" he asked. "All right. We'll just see who has the last laugh. I will enroll in cooking school."

"You're kidding!" Nancy stared at him. Ned's jaw was locked tight with determination. She blinked. "You're *not* kidding."

"Better yet," Ned said, warming to the challenge, "I'll enroll in the Claude DuPres International Cooking School and become a French chef."

"You?" Rick shook his head. "They'll never let you in."

"Oh, yeah?" Ned said. "My mother has a friend who enrolled in a six-week course and came back an expert. I've got the rest of the summer to kill. I'll do it."

"If you're really serious, I'll enroll too," Nancy said. "In fact, we can all do it! What about you guys?" she asked, glancing around at her friends.

George and Bess looked at each other. Then Bess turned to Ned and asked, "Is there a pastry class?"

George snorted. "Pastry class. Didn't you just start a new diet?"

"It can wait another six weeks," Bess retorted.

"What about you, George?" Nancy asked. "Let's all go."

"Are you kidding? I have tennis lessons to give."

"Hah!" Bess jeered. "You said yourself that that Matthews kid would like to take your place."

George glanced from one to the other of them. "Oh, all right," she grumbled. "If Ned Nickerson can go to cooking school, so can I." George shook back her short, dark hair. "I'll see if Matthews can substitute for me."

"Good!" Nancy said. "It's settled. Now all we have to do is get into the next class."

"I'll take care of that tomorrow. We should be ready to roll by next Monday," said Ned. "I don't want anyone chickening out."

As if they had rehearsed it, everyone turned and stared at the remains of the chicken.

Later that night, after everyone had left full of pizza, Nancy walked Ned to his car. "You're sure you want to go through with this?" she asked as Ned climbed into his car.

He nodded, rolling down his window. "I'll make the arrangements tomorrow. If we're lucky, we can leave on Monday."

Nancy leaned her elbows on the door. "Did anyone ever tell you you're a great guy?" she asked softly.

"I think George did, awhile back."

"Besides George." She tilted her head and

stared into his dark eyes. "I guess I'm just trying to say thanks."

"For what?" Ned looked genuinely puzzled.

"Just for being you." Nancy kissed him, then reluctantly pulled back.

"Monday," Ned said, and she nodded. As she dashed up the front porch steps, she heard him give her a farewell honk.

Nancy swept back her hair and squinted through the windshield of Ned's car. "Turn here," she said.

"I hope we have time to hit the showers," George said. "It's so hot and sticky."

"I don't think we will," Ned answered. He checked his watch. "There's an orientation meeting this afternoon—in fifteen minutes actually—and a short class afterward. We're lucky we got into the school at all."

"*And* into this hotel," Nancy said, staring up at the twin towers of the Westerly Hotel. "We're close enough to walk to the cooking school from here."

The girl at the desk assigned them their rooms. "You three are in the south tower," she said to Nancy, Bess, and George, handing them their keys. "And you, sir," she added, turning to Ned, "are in the north."

"I'm afraid we'll have to see our rooms later. We'd better head straight for the school," Nancy said, examining the map of the school grounds. Once outside she pointed in the direction they were to walk.

"Let's get going," she said, "or we'll be late."

They pushed through the hotel's rear doors and hurried past a courtyard with stone benches and fountains, and under a walkway. The famous cooking school could be glimpsed across and down the street.

Nancy and her friends raced into the main reception area of the school with just minutes to spare. At the auditorium, the first person they ran into was Claude DuPres himself.

A gray-haired man with florid cheeks, he welcomed them all individually.

"You will enjoy my school," he said. "You will learn to become master chefs if you work hard. Which classes are you taking, Ms. Drew?" he asked, reading her name tag.

Nancy smiled. Chef DuPres's heavy French accent was just what she would have expected from a world-renowned chef. "Ned and I are signed up for introductory French cooking," she said.

"Excellent. It's good to learn the basics. What about you?" he asked, turning to Bess and George.

"Pastry," Bess said promptly. "I can't wait."

"She sure can't," said George. "She couldn't stop talking about it in the car. I'm signed up for introductory Chinese cooking."

"I wish you all the best of luck," the chef told them.

Ned squeezed Nancy's hand. "Think you'll pick up cooking as fast as you learned to be a detective?"

Claude DuPres turned sharply in Nancy's direction. "You are a detective?"

Before Nancy could say anything, Bess jumped in. "Nancy's the best," she said loyally. "She's solved dozens of cases. I'm surprised you haven't heard of her."

"Bess!" Nancy said, embarrassed.

DuPres frowned. He seemed about to say something more, but he was interrupted by another wave of students entering the forum.

Nancy, Ned, Bess, and George moved into the auditorium. The place was so crowded they had difficulty finding two seats together.

Claude DuPres walked to the center of the stage and pulled up a wheeled cart. From a lower shelf he lifted several trays of delicate hors d'oeuvres and pastries. The class gave a collective sigh of envy.

"These are just samples from Chef Paul Slesak's pastry class," the chef told them. "The hors d'oeuvres were made by the students of another class. They are pretty, but easy to make."

DuPres lifted one of the pastries to his lips. "You will all learn this and much, much more. You will learn to be master chefs!" With a flourish he popped the tiny confection into his mouth.

"The sign-up sheets will be outside the doors of the classrooms. Classes are listed here." He held up a stack of papers, then handed them to a student who began passing them out. "When you arrive at your rooms—"

Claude DuPres never finished what he was about to say. With a strangled cry he suddenly fell forward over the cart and then slid in a heap to the floor!

Chapter Two

FOR HALF A beat nobody moved. Then Nancy and Ned rushed forward, and the place exploded with noise.

Nancy had just reached the unconscious DuPres when one of the other chefs, a thin man with a mustache, roughly pushed her aside. He dropped his ear to DuPres's chest.

"He has a weak heart," the man explained tersely. "Give him some air!"

Ned held up his hand to keep the crowd back and shouted, "Someone call an ambulance! I think Chef DuPres's having a heart attack!"

George took off like a shot. Nancy bent down to the mustached man. "Is there anything I can do?" she asked.

The man had undone the top buttons of DuPres's shirt and was looking down at the head of the cooking school. To her horror Nancy saw that DuPres's face had taken on a grayish tinge. His chest was rising and sinking shallowly. "I do not know what we can do," the man said in what sounded like a German accent.

Quickly Nancy read the pin attached to the man's lapel. Paul Slesak, it said. He must be the pastry chef DuPres had mentioned.

DuPres shuddered and moaned faintly. His eyelids fluttered open, and his gaze fixed determinedly on Nancy. "They—are—after—me," he muttered with difficulty.

"Shhh," Nancy said, alarmed. "You mustn't talk."

"Please—help me—"

"Chef DuPres!" Nancy exclaimed, but he was slipping back into unconsciousness.

She stared at him. A dozen questions were racing through her mind. What had he meant? Could this be something more than a heart attack?

Standing up abruptly, Paul Slesak grabbed Nancy's elbow. "Do not make him talk," he said flatly. "It is dangerous."

"I wasn't trying to—"

"Go." Chef Slesak waved her away dramatically. "I will attend to him."

Rudely he shouldered her aside, and just then the ambulance attendants arrived. They quickly moved DuPres to a stretcher and out the door to the waiting ambulance.

Paul Slesak moved forward. "Please! Everyone to your classes to meet your instructors," he said loudly. "Today's classes will proceed on schedule."

"What about Mr. DuPres?" a young man called.

"He is in good hands. Please. Go to your classrooms. That is all."

Nancy frowned. Was it her imagination, or was there a hint of satisfaction in Slesak's manner?

Feeling her steady gaze, Slesak turned to Nancy. "Is there something I can do for you?" he asked her coldly.

Nancy straightened. "I was just worried about Chef DuPres."

"He has had these attacks before. It will pass."

"You seem awfully sure of that."

Slesak didn't bother to answer her. He stalked off the stage and pushed through the doors to the outer corridor, leaving Nancy staring after him.

Ned had been keeping the crowd back. Now he returned to Nancy's side, touching her elbow. "You ready to go to class?"

"Yes, I guess so." She turned to him. "Ned, what's your impression of Slesak?"

He shrugged. "He handled that crisis pretty well."

"I suppose. But we have only Slesak's word that DuPres has a weak heart."

"That guy really bugged you, didn't he?" Ned asked.

"Yes, he did. Hang on a minute, Ned. I want to talk to Bess."

When Nancy caught up with her, Bess asked, "What are you doing here? I thought you were in Ned's class."

"I am. But I want you to do something for me."

"Uh-oh. What?"

"Paul Slesak will be teaching your class, and I don't trust him. He seems too—too—" Nancy finally shook her head in frustration. "Oh, I don't know. Too smug, I guess. Would you keep your eye on him for me? Let me know if anything strange goes on?"

"Don't tell me there's another mystery underfoot." Bess gave an exaggerated sigh. "I should have known."

"Thanks, Bess. I owe you one." Nancy laughed and dashed off to find Ned.

He was waiting impatiently by the door of their classroom. "Hurry up," he said. "Everyone's inside already."

"I wonder who the instructor is," Nancy whispered as she slipped into the back of the room. The students were standing in a semicircle around a half-dozen sinks, a refrigerator, three rows of counters, several range tops, and an enormous gas oven.

A young chef was standing by the oven. "Everyone please put on an apron and hat," the chef said, his tone flat and disinterested. "Women, if you have long hair, tuck it inside your hats or pull it back." He heaved a sigh and glanced at his watch.

As Nancy pulled her hair into a ponytail, she wondered why the young chef sounded so bored. *It's as if he doesn't really want us here,* she thought.

The young chef introduced himself as Trent Richards, an assistant chef working to become a master chef. He was an American, and he made a point of telling them all about himself.

"I'm just finishing my courses here, and then I'll be on my way to the big time," Richards said, by way of wrapping up his introductory speech.

"Humble sort of guy, isn't he?" Ned muttered, tying on his apron.

Nancy and Ned sat down on stools behind the rear counter, and Chef Richards launched into a speech about the cooking school. But before long he returned to talking about himself.

"I hope he gets all this out of his system today," Ned said under his breath. "The guy's a broken record!"

Nancy had to agree. Richards just didn't seem like much of a teacher. And he looked even less like a chef. He was tall and gangly, and right then he was staring over their heads toward the door.

"Now, first things first," Richards said. "In the cupboards in front of your stools are all the tools you'll need."

While the students looked through their cupboards, Nancy saw Richards consult his watch again. He's done that several times, she realized. Is he in a hurry to meet someone? Or just bored?

"Come on, come on," he said irritably. "We haven't got all day."

Nancy bent down to search her cupboard. "Paul Slesak and Trent Richards sure aren't going to win any personality contests," she whispered to Ned as she hurriedly placed her utensils on the stainless steel counter.

"Maybe it's something they ate."

They burst into silent laughter—but stopped abruptly when Richards glared at them.

The young chef began fiddling with the calibrated dials for the gas oven. When nothing happened, he muttered angrily, "Terrific. The pilot light's out again. I'll have to relight it."

As the class watched, Richards opened an underpanel. Then he struck a match and reached in to reignite the pilot light.

There was a loud *whoomph!* and blue flames exploded from the oven. Richards stumbled backward, his sleeve smoldering. Frantically he tried to beat out the sparks with his other hand.

It was no use. In front of Nancy's eyes, flames leapt up and licked at Richards's arm. In another minute the fire would engulf him!

Chapter Three

SOMEONE IN THE class screamed. Chef Richards's arm was ablaze, and acrid smoke was filling the room. "Help me!" Richards shouted frantically.

"The fire extinguisher!" Ned yelled, yanking it off the wall.

Then abruptly the flames shooting from the oven vanished—as if someone had turned off a spigot. But Chef Richards's jacket was still burning.

"Look out!" Ned shouted. He shot a stream of

white foam onto the chef's arm, and the fire died instantly.

"Are you all right?" Nancy asked Richards, who looked dazed.

"It's not too bad," he said, staring down at his arms. His jacket was ruined. Huge holes were singed through to his shirt beneath.

"Are you sure?" Nancy asked.

"I'm fine," Richards said. He yanked off his coat and rolled up the sleeves of his shirt. The skin beneath was red, as if he'd been in the sun too long.

"You're lucky it's not any worse," Nancy said quietly.

"Better get away from that oven," Ned told Richards.

"The oven's fine now," Richards said flatly. "The gas is off. The pilot light isn't even on."

"How can that be?" Nancy asked. "It was on just a moment ago."

"Was it?" Richards gave her an unreadable look.

"Well, yes. That's how the fire got started, isn't it?"

Color was returning to the chef's pale cheeks. It flooded over his face in an angry dark-red wave. "Yeah, right. That's how it got started," he spit out. He brushed past her and charged out of the room.

Nancy followed him into the hallway. "Are you leaving? What should we do?"

"Stay there." He waved her back. "I'll send someone along."

When Nancy walked back into the room, Ned was bending over the oven. "Maybe everyone should go out to the hall," she suggested.

"No, it's all right." Ned stood up, wiping the oily grime from his hand onto his white apron. "Richards was right. The pilot light's out, and there's no gas leak."

There was a collective sigh of relief from the class. Nancy walked to Ned's side, staring at the oven.

"Then what started the fire?" she asked, chewing on her lower lip.

"Uh-oh," Ned said. "I recognize that look on your face."

"What look?"

"That on-the-trail-of-a-mystery look. I don't think your mind's on cooking."

"There might be something more going on here than meets the eye," Nancy said. "First Claude DuPres collapses in the auditorium, and now an oven bursts into flame. A pretty unusual first day, wouldn't you say?"

"Well, yeah, when you put it that way." Ned looked thoughtful.

Just then another chef walked into the room. Nancy glanced his way—and did a double take. The new chef wasn't much older than she was, and he was the stuff dreams were made of: tall, dark, and handsome, with a rakish smile and brooding gray eyes. She looked at Ned, who whispered in her ear, "You always get upset when I look at girls the way you're looking at him."

Nancy's blue eyes sparkled. "Just because I'm on a diet doesn't mean I can't look at the menu."

"One more cooking joke and you're history," Ned groaned.

The new chef strode to the front of the room as the students sat down again. Placing his palms flat on the counter, he had to duck his head to see the class from beneath the wrought-iron pot rack that swung from the ceiling. "Well," he said with a smile. "I understand there's been some excitement around here today.

"My name is Jacques Bonet." He introduced himself in a voice that had only a trace of a French accent. "I'll fill in for Chef Richards today. This was a frightening accident. And until the oven is checked out and repaired, we won't use it."

Nancy could tell that Bonet wanted to get back to a business-as-usual atmosphere. He opened the cupboard in front of him and pulled out a skillet. "To understand French cuisine, you must first understand what makes a good sauce. Let me demonstrate."

He turned on one of the burners and slid a fat pat of butter expertly around in a shallow pan until it had melted. Then he tossed in some flour. For a minute or two he worked the butter and flour together with a whisk, then lifted the pan from the gas flame. "This is called a roux," he explained. "A mixture of fat and flour. It is important that the roux be mixed well, or the sauce will be lumpy when the liquid is added."

Deftly he added two cups of milk. The mixture sizzled enticingly. "Keep stirring constantly," Bonet warned, "or your sauce will burn and stick to the bottom. Especially if you add milk. Milk has milk sugar—lactose—in it, and sugar burns easily."

Ned glanced from Bonet to Nancy. "You need a degree in chemistry for this!"

Overhearing him, Bonet said, "Courses in chemistry are almost a must for a true master chef. One cannot understand why food reacts as it does without breaking it down into its particular elements. *Voilà!*" He finished and placed the pan with the smooth, creamy white sauce on the tile counter. "It is *fini!*"

"I've made lots of sauces before," a girl said. "But I never knew why I did what I did."

"Tomorrow you will all get a chance to make your own sauce. That is all for today."

The rest of the class began to file out, but Nancy paused by the door. "I want to ask Chef Bonet a few questions about Trent Richards," she murmured to Ned.

Nancy walked slowly back to where Bonet was clearing off the counter. What was the best way to get the information she wanted? "When is someone coming to fix the oven?" she asked.

"Probably this evening. Or maybe tomorrow morning." Bonet sounded unconcerned. "The school has a maintenance man who will see to the oven as soon as he can."

Smearing some of the blackened grime from the oven onto her finger, Nancy rubbed it thoughtfully with her thumb. "Chef Richards seemed kind of concerned about the accident."

"I imagine he was," Bonet answered soberly.

"No, I mean he acted as if he wasn't totally surprised it had happened."

"What do you mean?" the chef asked, straightening up to stare at her.

"I don't know exactly. Could it be that the pilot light wasn't really the problem? Could the accident have been caused by something else?" Or someone else, she thought to herself.

Jacques's gray eyes searched Nancy's. He seemed to take a good hard look at her for the first time—and it was obvious he liked what he saw. Reading her name tag, he asked, "What are you getting at, Mademoiselle Drew?"

"I'm a detective—" she started to explain.

Ned, who had been walking slowly across the room toward them, interrupted her. "She likes to get to the bottom of things."

"Are you a *professional* detective?" Bonet asked incredulously.

"Amateur."

Bonet was silent for a long time. Then he inclined his head. "Well, in that case I think the best thing for you to do is talk to Trent. I'm not sure where he is right now, but you can check with the main office."

Before Nancy could ask any more questions, Ned's hand had clamped around her arm. He steered her firmly out of the room.

"What do you think you're doing?" she demanded, shaking off his hand.

"Trying to save your neck! If there's really something going on around here, you'd better be careful whom you confide in."

"Confide in? You mean Chef Bonet? I was just asking him some questions."

"I don't really like him. Just who is he, anyway? He's pretty young to be a master chef."

"Trent Richards is young," Nancy pointed out.

"But he's not of Bonet's caliber."

"We don't know that. Richards didn't get a chance to show us what he knew."

"Well, Bonet sure did," Ned muttered.

Nancy couldn't help smiling. "Are you a little jealous? Would it help if I said he isn't my type?"

Ned was about to protest. Then he seemed to think better of it. "Yeah," he grumbled. "It would help a lot."

"He's not my type."

Ned laughed in spite of himself, and they left the cooking school and walked back to the hotel.

They met Bess and George in the main lobby.

Bess was reading a pamphlet whose pages were covered with pictures of pastry. "Tomorrow we get into dough. I mean, really into dough," she said rapturously. "Puff pastry with Bavarian cream filling." Bess closed her eyes in mock ecstasy. "This is what I call heaven."

"Hog heaven," George remarked, which earned her a withering glance from Bess.

"Did anything exciting happen in your classes?" Nancy asked. Both girls shook their heads. "Ours was a real doozy," Nancy added. Quickly she filled them in on what had happened with the oven.

"Nancy thinks there's some kind of mystery going on," Ned told them. "This school seems a little too accident-prone."

"*And* there was Claude DuPres's remark about someone being after him," Nancy reminded them. "I wish I knew how he was doing."

"Why not call the office?" George suggested. "Maybe they've heard from the hospital."

"Good idea. I'll see if I can find out where Trent Richards is too."

Nancy went to a pay phone and called the office. The receptionist told her that there had been no word on Chef DuPres's progress. He was being carefully watched at the hospital, and he had definitely had a heart attack. When Nancy asked how she could contact Trent Richards, the receptionist told her that she wasn't at liberty to give out his address.

"I guess I'll have to wait and talk to Richards tomorrow," Nancy said, returning to their group.

Bess rubbed her eyes. "I'm bushed. Let's get something to eat and then go to bed early."

"Good idea," said Ned.

They ate dinner at the hotel coffee shop, but Nancy didn't have much of an appetite. Her head was too full of the events of the day. She kept thinking about Chef DuPres and Trent Richards.

A heart attack and an unforeseeable accident. But was that all that was going on?

After dinner Ned walked them toward the south tower and to the glass elevator that led to the upper floors. "See you tomorrow," he said.

"Right. Tomorrow," Nancy answered distractedly.

"Still thinking about the fire?"

Nancy sighed. "Yeah. Among other things. You know, Chef DuPres collapsed right after he ate that hors d'oeuvre. Do you suppose . . . ?" She left the thought unfinished.

"Didn't the school tell you it was something to do with his heart?" Bess asked.

"Yes, but he was afraid. I distinctly heard him beg for help." Nancy shook her head. "And then that fire in our classroom and the way Richards reacted." Nancy turned to Ned. "He got mad, remember? He raced out as if he were ready to tear somebody apart."

"Come on," George said. "Let's hit the sack.

I've got another big day of chopping and slicing ahead."

Ned kissed Nancy and said goodbye. Then the elevator doors closed in front of the three girls' faces. The elevator whizzed upward, and soon they were on the seventeenth floor.

"This hotel is really nice," George said sleepily as she unlocked the door to the room she was sharing with Bess. "Lucky we got a reduced rate through the cooking school."

"My room's right next door," Nancy said, unlocking her own door. "I'll knock on the connecting door and wake you guys up in the morning."

As Bess followed George inside their room, Nancy heard George warn her cousin, "Just don't leave your makeup all over the bathroom counter this time."

"You worry about the silliest things," Bess answered with a yawn. Then the door closed behind them.

Nancy smiled. She wished either Bess or George would give up the idea of sleep and come talk to her. She wasn't the least bit tired.

She sat up for a while, reading. Her stomach started to rumble, and she was thirsty. Well, she decided, there had to be a soda machine nearby.

Nancy stepped into the elevator and it sped to the ground floor. After finding a soda machine and drinking half a can, she still didn't feel like returning to her room. Instead she wandered around the hotel lobby, thinking about the events of the day.

When she noticed a sign pointing the way to the sun deck and pool, Nancy decided to head that way. It was too late for a swim, but maybe she'd be able to find a place to sit and think and watch the water.

She was heading down the corridor marked Pool when she heard two men talking. Her heart beat faster. One of the voices belonged to Trent Richards!

"I want a bigger piece of the pie," he was saying coldly. "And don't try any more stunts like that one today, or I'll put you out of the way for good!"

Chapter Four

A BIGGER PIECE of the pie! Nancy ran on tiptoe to the corner of the hall, straining to hear more. Something really was going on! Trent Richards was in the thick of something sinister.

The other man's voice was indistinguishable. Did it have a French accent? Nancy leaned forward as far as she dared without stepping into the connecting hallway, but she couldn't keep her heel from scraping against the wall.

"What was that?" Trent demanded. "Someone's there!"

Sudden silence. Then footsteps quickly retreating. Nancy peeked around the corner, but all she saw was the exit door at the end of the hall slowly closing.

She had to find out whom Trent was threatening!

Nancy yanked open the door—and stopped short. Stairs led both up and down. She listened carefully and heard a door click softly shut in the basement.

Nancy raced down the stairs and thrust open the door. She climbed up three steps and found herself outside in the warm night. There was no breeze, and the air was thick with humidity. Neither Trent Richards nor his companion was anywhere in sight.

Nancy stood quietly in the shadows, listening for any hint of their voices, but her quarry was long gone.

The classroom was full by the time Nancy slipped through the door the following day. She grabbed her apron and hat and found her place beside Ned.

Nancy glanced around. "Hi. Is Richards back?"

"No one's shown up yet."

At that moment the door opened and Jacques Bonet entered. "Looks as though I'm filling in for Chef Richards again today," he said with a smile as he walked to the front.

"What happened to Chef Richards?" Nancy asked. "Is he all right?"

"He's fine. He just asked for a couple of days off. Now, I want everyone to make a white sauce, just as I did yesterday."

There was no time for further questions. Nancy would have to push the mystery aside for a while and concentrate on cooking.

She and Ned were working together on one range top. While Nancy looked on, Ned measured off a square of butter and dropped it into the hot skillet. It started sizzling wildly and instantly turned brown.

"Quick, get the skillet off the burner!" Nancy said.

Ned slid it to one side, but it was too late. The smell of burned butter wafted up from the pan. "Great," he said between his teeth.

"Can I help?"

Turning, Nancy saw Jacques Bonet's handsome face within inches of hers. "Uh—yeah," she said. "I guess." She moved back and watched as Jacques helped Ned get started again. This time the butter melted slowly, but as Ned dumped the flour in, Bonet shook his head.

"Too much flour," the young chef told Ned. "Some people would try to add more butter, but me—" He spread his hands. "I would start over." As Ned groaned, Jacques turned to Nancy. "Perhaps your pretty friend would like a try?"

Feeling put on the spot, Nancy cut off a fat wedge of butter and skimmed it around the bottom of the hot pan. When it was melted, she added some flour.

"A bit more, I think," Bonet said, so close to her ear that Nancy could feel his breath on her hair.

She shook in more flour, then quickly whisked the mixture together until the flour was completely covered with butter.

"Now add the milk to the roux," Jacques said, handing her the cup.

Nancy poured in the milk. The liquid hissed and bubbled. Quickly she lifted the skillet from the flame, afraid it would burn.

"Go on," Jacques urged. "You're doing fine."

Nancy started whisking again and kept going until she could see the sauce begin to thicken. When it was done she was pleased to hear Jacques say, "*Voilà!* Miss Drew, that is excellent.

"Now, Mr. Nickerson. Try again and pay attention to proportions."

When the chef walked over to the next group of students, Ned let out a pent-up breath. And Nancy waited quietly while he tried again. She glanced at the clock. The morning was almost over.

"I want to ask Bonet a few more questions about Trent Richards," Nancy said to Ned. "I think I'm missing something important."

"Me too." Ned's gaze was glued to the melting

butter. "There!" he said in satisfaction as it pooled evenly on the bottom of the skillet.

Nancy gave him a quick smile. "Now you're cooking. I'll go talk to Bonet." She waited until Bonet had finished helping some other students. "Excuse me," she said when he glanced her way. "I was wondering if I could talk to you for a few minutes."

"Sure." He smiled. "What's on your mind?"

Nancy took a deep breath. She wanted information, and for that she needed to gain the man's confidence. Maybe a little flattery was in order. "Well, I'm just so impressed with your skills as a chef," she gushed. "You must have quite a reputation."

"Well, yes." His smile grew wider. "I do."

"Since Chef DuPres is in the hospital, are you in charge then?"

The chef laughed. "I may have the skills, but not the years. Paul Slesak is Claude's replacement."

"You mean, Chef Slesak knew he would be Chef DuPres's replacement if anything happened to DuPres?"

Bonet nodded. "Paul was the one who asked me to fill in for Trent."

"I see," Nancy said slowly. "Then normally you're in charge of something else here?"

"Actually, no. I'm a guest chef at the school. I travel to a lot of different cooking schools around the world, but Claude DuPres is a close friend of mine. I wanted to help him out." He lifted his shoulders dismissively. "Claude has an office for me, but I prefer to move around."

"You know Chef DuPres personally?"

"He is my . . ." He broke off, searching for the right word.

"Mentor?" Nancy suggested.

"Oui." Bonet's smile was a slash of white in his dark face. "My mentor. He taught me to be the best."

"How is Chef DuPres?"

Bonet shot her a quick glance. Had he suddenly realized she was pumping him for information? "The last I heard he was doing fine," he said in a clipped voice.

"I hope he's all right," Nancy said sincerely. "Well, I'd better go see how Ned's doing," Nancy murmured.

As quickly as she could, she returned to Ned's side. He was diligently stirring milk into his roux, but lumps were starting to form anyway.

"Not enough fat to coat the starch molecules in the flour," Jacques said, coming up behind them.

Ned glanced sideways at Jacques. He looked about ready to explode.

Unaware, Jacques turned to address the whole class. "Many of you are having problems with proportions. I would like you to master this roux now," Bonet said, striding to the center of the room, "because I want everyone to make a Béarnaise sauce after lunch. The recipes are here. You can study them during your break." He held up a sheaf of papers. Then he turned and looked at Nancy, smiling at her.

While the students picked up their recipes, Ned growled in Nancy's ear, "I'm liking that guy less and less."

"Shhh," Nancy said. "I might need some information out of him."

"He's interested in a whole lot more than information from you."

Nancy looked up at him, smiling. "Well, I'm spoken for. But can *you* hold it together? I don't want to blow this."

"Just what are you hoping to learn?"

"Jacques told me he's a close friend of Claude DuPres's. Maybe he can give some clue as to what's going on here."

"Whatever that is," Ned said.

"Whatever that is," Nancy repeated.

The afternoon class was embarrassing for Nancy. Over and over Jacques praised her profusely. She could practically feel the other students' resentment. Even Ned was having a hard time not losing his cool.

When class was over, Nancy was glad to escape to the hallway. "Whew!" she exclaimed to herself, stopping to wait for Ned.

But it was Jacques who caught up with her first. He clasped both her hands in his.

"Would you be my guest for dinner tonight?" he asked. "There's an authentic French restaurant on the other side of the city. Even I can't fault the food."

"I—I—uh—" Nancy cleared her throat. "Thank you for the invitation, Mr. Bonet, but—"

"Jacques. Please call me Jacques."

"All right—Jacques. But I already have plans with my friends for this evening."

Ned was right behind them now. He snapped his fingers in mock regret. "Too bad. Maybe another time."

"Hey, you guys!" came a voice from down the hall. It was Bess, running toward them and waving frantically.

"Nancy, guess what?" Bess asked breathlessly.

"What?"

"I made the best éclair in class. You wouldn't believe it. It was just perfect. . . ." Her voice trailed off. She's noticed Jacques, Nancy thought, smiling to herself.

"Jacques, this is my friend, Bess Marvin," Nancy said. "Bess, Jacques Bonet."

"Bonjour," said Jacques—and Nancy could practically see Bess melt.

"Chef Bonet is our instructor," Nancy said.

"You're a chef?" Bess's eyes widened.

"Yes, I am. I just asked Nancy to join me for

dinner, but she told me she's already going out with her friends. Would that be you?"

"Yes. But you could come with us!" Bess said eagerly. "Right?" She turned to Nancy for confirmation.

"Uh, sure," Nancy said. She was aware of Ned's mounting tension, but she couldn't do anything about it. Bess had pretty much forced Nancy into inviting Jacques along. "Why don't you join us, Jacques? Are you staying at the hotel too?"

He nodded. "I will meet you in the lobby. Say, around six?"

Bess grabbed Nancy's arm as soon as Jacques was out of earshot. "Who is that guy, really? He's too gorgeous to be a chef!"

"Who said chefs can't be gorgeous?" Nancy countered, shooting Ned a glance.

"I can't wait for dinner!" Bess responded with feeling.

Nancy linked her arm through Ned's, but all the way to the hotel, he didn't utter one word.

After Bess headed straight up to her room to change, Nancy said to Ned, "Wait a sec. I want to talk to you."

"About what?"

"Jacques Bonet! You don't seriously think I'm interested in him, do you?"

"No," Ned admitted. "But he's definitely interested in you."

Nancy couldn't deny that. "Well, it bothers me

too," she said. "I can't afford to antagonize him at this stage, but I'd just as soon he didn't use me as an example in class. I think I'm losing friends."

To her relief, Ned hugged her. "You haven't lost this one yet. But one more perfect sauce and—" He drew his finger across his neck.

Nancy laughed, gave him a quick kiss, then hurried upstairs. In her room she changed into a pair of jeans, a tank top, and a gauzy peach-colored overshirt.

When they all met once again in the lobby, Jacques was already there. George whistled softly under her breath. "That's your instructor?" she asked incredulously.

Nancy could understand George's amazement. Jacques had been handsome enough in his white chef's uniform. Now, in a pair of washed-out black jeans and a black shirt, Jacques Bonet looked even more handsome—and a little dangerous. Not like a chef at all.

"So where are we going to eat?" Bess asked, once Nancy had introduced Jacques to George.

"I'm dying for a burger and fries," George answered. Without much discussion they decided to hit the nearest fast-food burger place.

Jacques didn't say anything until they had actually walked inside. He searched the menu carefully and waited until the others had ordered. Then he bought a salad for himself.

"You don't like hamburgers?" Ned asked in disbelief.

Jacques grimaced. "Would you expect a chef to eat fast food?" he asked.

Bess was staring at Jacques, starry-eyed. "Next time we'll pick a place you'll like better," she said. "What made you decide to become a chef?"

"It was really Claude's influence. I had originally wanted a more exciting career for myself."

"Such as?" Nancy asked.

His smile was reflective. "I don't know. Something with a little more danger. Such as being a detective." He broke off and stared straight into Nancy's eyes.

Her face growing hot, Nancy cleared her throat and changed the subject. "Did you find out any more about Chef DuPres's condition?" she asked.

"He had a mild heart attack, but he's doing fine. In fact, he's due to be released from the hospital in a day or two."

Nancy could hardly believe it. Was that all that had been the matter?

"You seem surprised," Jacques remarked.

"Oh, no. I'm glad. It's just that—I don't know. I was just worried, I guess," Nancy stammered.

"About what?"

"About Chef DuPres, of course! Anyone want dessert?"

* * *

Back in the lobby, Nancy said, "Well, thanks for joining us, Jacques." She thrust out her hand to shake his.

Instead of shaking it, Jacques brought it to his lips, kissing it softly on the palm.

"The pleasure was all mine," he said huskily.

There was a sudden sound behind him. Nancy looked up. Oh, no! she thought.

Ned's fist was aimed, ready to smash into Jacques's handsome face!

Chapter Five

JACQUES MOVED OUT of the way so quickly that Ned never had a chance to hit him.

Ned's fingers relaxed. "You move pretty fast," he observed.

"I've met jealous boyfriends before," Jacques said, panting slightly. His tone was light, but underneath was a hard edge.

"Then you might try keeping your hands to yourself," Ned snarled.

"Hey, wait a minute!" Nancy said. "Come on, guys, let's call it a night. This is really getting out of hand."

After a moment Jacques inclined his head. "See you tomorrow," he said, then he strode off down the hall.

The four friends stared after him for a second. Then Ned turned to Nancy. "Am I crazy? Or do you understand how I feel?"

"*I* understand how you feel," George said. "That guy's so smooth he glides."

Bess's mouth dropped open. "What do you mean? I think he's cute."

Everyone groaned. Nancy linked her arm through Ned's. "He does come on a little strong," she said softly. "But please hang in there, okay? Don't antagonize him. I know this is all really awkward, but we might need a friend later."

"That guy is nobody's friend," Ned muttered. "You're the boss, Nan. But so help me, if he steps out of line . . ." He left the threat unfinished.

"You'll get first crack at him," Nancy assured him. She just hoped it would never come to that.

Inside her room Nancy brushed her teeth and changed into her nightshirt. She walked out of the bathroom to find a pajama-clad George sitting cross-legged on her bed.

"Do you really think this Jacques can help you figure out what's going on here?" George asked skeptically.

"Yes, I do. He's right in the center of it all."

"The center of what?"

"I don't know!" Nancy stared at her reflection in the mirror over the bureau. "I just wish I did."

Just then Bess padded into the room. "That Jacques is gorgeous! And he's so—gallant!"

"Forget Jacques for a minute," Nancy said. "Think about that oven that caught fire. Trent Richards acted really strange about that." She turned to Bess. "Did Paul Slesak do or say anything odd or suspicious today?"

Bess shook her head. "My class was just a class. Did I tell you I made the best—"

"Twice," George said.

It was getting late, and Nancy decided it was time to forget about the mystery. "Let's hit the hay," she suggested. "Tomorrow's another day."

Bess and George slipped through the connecting door to their room, and Nancy crawled into bed. She had thought she might have trouble getting to sleep again, but that night she fell asleep instantly.

She awoke early the next morning, had a quick shower, then dressed in a pair of tan jeans and a white T-shirt. "Rise and shine," she called to her friends through the connecting door.

George's answer was a pillow hurled against the wall beside Nancy. Bess didn't move. "I'll meet you both later," Nancy said, and ducked before George could hurl another missile.

Downstairs, Nancy checked her watch. She

had a lot of time until class started. She strolled over to the hotel coffee shop and sat down at a small table in the corner. Might as well let Ned get his beauty sleep, she thought with a wry smile.

She'd just ordered a bowl of fresh fruit when a familiar voice with a French accent said, "Fancy meeting you here."

Nancy glanced up into the gray eyes of Jacques Bonet. "Oh, hi," she said.

"Mind if I join you?" he asked.

"Uh, no. Sure. Go ahead."

Jacques sat down opposite her. "Black coffee," he told the waitress. Then he just stared at Nancy. She could hardly swallow under such close scrutiny.

"It's only six-thirty, but you look wide-awake," she said, trying to sound offhand.

"I've been up since five, working out."

"Five? How can you stand it?"

"Habit, I guess. I've got to keep in shape somehow."

"Well, I'd never be able to— Oh, there's Ned!" He was standing at the entrance to the coffee shop. Nancy called to him and beckoned him over.

Ned walked slowly to their table, but his voice was friendly as he asked, "Well, what have you got in store for us today, Chef Bonet?"

"I thought we would try a soufflé."

"Soufflé, huh?" Ned eyed Jacques over the top of his menu.

"Soufflés are difficult for amateurs," Jacques said. "But once you learn the basics, it's a snap."

"Well, I hope you're right," Nancy said.

While Ned ordered a hearty breakfast, Jacques excused himself. He sounded a little disgruntled when he left. Was he angry that Ned was there?

When they got to class Jacques put them right to work making soufflés. "You need to whip the egg whites hard and fast," Jacques said to the room at large. "The more air you whip into them, the fluffier the soufflé." He casually dropped a hand on Nancy's shoulder. "How is it going?"

Ned, who was taking a turn with the wire whip, was beating the whites so fast and furiously Nancy was afraid they might take flight. "Uh—fine," she said, sliding away from Jacques.

When the handsome instructor finally moved on to the next students, Ned relaxed a little. "Don't say it," he warned. "That guy is specifically trying to get to me."

"Then don't let him."

"Oh, yeah? Easy for you to say. You're not the one who has to watch."

"Well, maybe trying to make friends with him wasn't such a hot idea," Nancy admitted. "I haven't learned anything useful yet, and he's really bugging you."

"As long as you're not interested in him, I can take it," Ned said.

Jacques left them alone for most of the rest of class, and Nancy and Ned put together a cheese soufflé they could be proud of.

"If this thing deflates I'm giving up cooking and going back to chess," Ned said, watching the soufflé as if he expected it to disintegrate before his eyes.

"You've scared it," Nancy said. "It wouldn't dare deflate now."

Jacques walked over to them. "Well done!" he said heartily. "Some of the others are still finishing up, but I'm running out of supplies. There is a slab of bacon on a shelf inside the freezer. Would you mind getting it, Ned? The freezer's on the first floor. Go down the stairs, turn right, then go to the end of the corridor. You can't miss it."

Ned shot a dark look at Jacques, but he headed for the door anyway. "I'll call if I get lost," he said over his shoulder.

Nancy watched Ned go out the door. Then she turned to find Jacques smiling at her. "I thought Trent Richards was coming back," she said nervously.

"I'm not really sure what Trent's doing," Jacques answered. "I asked Paul this morning, but he hasn't heard from him."

"That's funny."

"Yes. It is." Jacques regarded her steadily.

"Nancy, I get the feeling you think Trent's disappearance is odd."

"Well, as a matter of fact—"

Nancy never got to finish her sentence. The door to the room burst open and Ned walked in, white faced. His breathing was ragged and fast, his chest heaving. Quickly Nancy stepped forward.

"Ned?" she asked, afraid. "What's wrong?"

"It's Richards," Ned gasped. "I've found him."

"Found him? What do you mean, *found* him?"

"He's in the freezer." Ned drew a deep breath, then exhaled slowly. "He's dead, Nancy. He's dead."

Chapter Six

"WHAT?" JACQUES DEMANDED, but Nancy was already bolting for the door.

Nancy raced down the stairs and charged around the corner. Her heart was pounding, but she had to see for herself.

The walk-in freezer was just where Jacques had said it would be. For a second Nancy hesitated at the door. Then she twisted the knob and stepped inside.

Sure enough, Trent Richards's body was lying on the floor, stashed behind some crates. Nancy had barely gotten a glance at him before Ned's arms closed around her and pulled her back outside.

An instant later Jacques Bonet appeared. "I have called the police," he said soberly. "This is one accident too many."

A crowd had already gathered by the time the police arrived. Ned had to describe over and over again how he'd found the body.

Nancy watched quietly as Richards's body was removed from the premises. Then she walked up to the nearest officer and asked, "What was the cause of death? Freezing?"

The officer in charge frowned at Nancy. "We'll have to wait for the coroner's report," he said. "All I can tell you is that there was a blow to his head, but we're listing his death as an accident."

"But there is a chance it wasn't an accident?" Nancy asked.

"Is there some reason you suspect foul play, miss?" the officer asked.

"Well, yes, as a matter of fact there is. A couple of nights ago I heard Trent Richards threaten someone. He wanted a 'bigger piece of the pie.' "

"But you didn't see his face?"

"No."

"You're sure it was a threat?"

"What else could it be?"

He snapped his notebook shut. "Now, don't take offense. But Richards was a chef. This 'piece of the pie' comment—could it have anything to do with cooking?"

Nancy tried not to be insulted. He doesn't know you're a detective, she reminded herself. "It was a threat," she said firmly. "He said, 'Or I'll put you out of the way for good.' "

The policeman shrugged. "Well, we'll look into it."

"Claude DuPres, the head of the DuPres cooking school, was threatened too. He thought someone was after him."

"He told you that?" the man asked swiftly.

"He murmured it just after his heart attack. He pleaded for help."

The officer looked thoughtful. He glanced quickly at her name tag and said, "Thank you, Ms. Drew," as he walked out. "I'll have to have a talk with Chef DuPres."

The next morning before class Nancy concluded that the only way to attack the mystery *was* to confront Claude DuPres. She felt certain he was the key, somehow. It was just a matter of being able to see him—and see him alone.

When she arrived for class, Nancy had barely scooted into her place beside Ned when he said, "Did you hear? Chef DuPres's out of the hospital. He's even back at school today—against his doctor's orders."

"Is that right?" Nancy asked excitedly.

"That's what everybody's been saying," Ned said. "I guess cooking's his life."

"Great. This is my chance to finally talk to him at lunch today."

"Maybe I should come with you."

Nancy shook her head. "No. Meet Bess and George and tell them what I'm doing. I'll be okay."

"That's what they all say," Ned muttered. But when lunchtime came he went to meet George and Bess as she headed for Chef DuPres's office.

The office was on the second floor of the adjacent building. Nancy hurried up the stairs, shoving her sunglasses to the top of her head. She checked her watch and made a face. She wasn't going to have much time to talk to him.

"Entrez!" Claude DuPres called when Nancy rapped at the door.

Nancy stuck her head inside the door. "Chef DuPres? My name's Nancy Drew. I met you on the first day of this class session, as we were all walking into the auditorium."

The chef's face was still ashen. He beckoned her feebly over to his desk. "I remember you, Ms. Drew. It was right before my—heart attack. You are the detective."

"How are you feeling?" Nancy asked.

"Much better. Though my doctor would like to chain me to my bed." His smile was wry.

"Do you remember what you said when you first came to?"

He froze, then shook his head.

"You said someone was after you. You asked for help."

DuPres averted his eyes. "You must have misunderstood."

"I couldn't have misunderstood. I was right there." Nancy stared at him. Why was he covering up?

"Ms. Drew, I was not myself that day. I may have said many things."

Nancy slowly sank into the chair across from his desk. She was certain DuPres remembered what he'd said. But how could she get him to open up?

She looked around the room for a minute, trying to think of what to say next. On the wall behind his desk were many pictures of the famed chef with famous people. To the far right hung a picture of half a dozen solemn-faced men, seated around a long table.

Claude DuPres's eyes followed her gaze, and his expression tightened. "There you see the real owners of the Claude DuPres International Cooking School," he said with a trace of irony. "I am more the—how do you say?—the up-front person?"

"You're the spokesman?" Nancy was startled. She had assumed the school belonged solely to him. "You mean you're not the owner?"

"I own a small percentage of the school, and I am on the board of directors." He shrugged. "I am paid for the use of my name and for my support of the school."

Nancy wondered if the board of directors would choose Paul Slesak to run the school if anything should happen to Claude DuPres. But would that be reason enough for Slesak to want DuPres out of the way? She couldn't ask that.

Choosing another tack, Nancy said, "I'm sure you've heard about Trent Richards."

DuPres's face grew sad. "A terrible, terrible accident. I cannot believe it could happen here."

"What if it wasn't an accident? What if someone tampered with the freezer door handle and locked Chef Richards in on purpose?" Nancy asked.

"What? What are you saying?"

Quickly Nancy related the series of events that had taken place, ending with Trent's threats to that unknown person.

"You are making this up!" the chef said angrily.

"Why would I? I don't think Chef Richards's death was an accident, and I don't think the oven's catching fire was an accident either."

DuPres shook his head, his hands nervously shuffling the papers in front of him. "It has nothing to do with me."

Nancy was sure he was hiding something. "What could Chef Richards have been involved in?" she asked, watching him closely. "Why would he be threatening someone?"

"He was not a popular chef," DuPres admitted reluctantly. "He was too interested in climbing to the top. Success was everything. He made that very clear."

"And he resented having to work for it," Nancy suggested, remembering Trent's attitude in class.

"Yes. He wanted too much, too soon." DuPres shrugged. "He was young."

"But that doesn't explain why he would—" Nancy started to say.

"Maybe you should forget these theories. Chef Richards's death was an unfortunate accident. That is all."

"And what about you?" she asked. "You said, 'They are after me.' Could 'they' have really been Trent Richards?"

"No!"

"Then who? Paul Slesak?"

He shook his head, his lips tight.

"Jacques Bonet?" Nancy suggested.

Claude DuPres shook his head rapidly. "You do not know what you are saying."

"I'm sorry, Chef DuPres," Nancy answered. "Please don't excite yourself."

"Excite myself? You accuse my friend Jacques—the one man I trust—when I know that it can only be—" He broke off, his eyes widening.

Nancy stood up and leaned over his desk, her sunglasses tipping from her crown. "It can only be who, Chef DuPres? Who?"

She held her breath, watching his face slowly drain of color. "I really do not know," he finally admitted. "I have only guesses. But, yes, Ms. Drew, someone has been threatening me."

"Do you have any idea why?"

"No." He shook his head. "But I do know one thing: if Trent Richards was murdered, the murderer made a mistake."

"A mistake?" Nancy asked, puzzled.

Claude DuPres drew a shaky breath. "Yes, a mistake. A very costly one. You see, the murderer was really after *me.*"

Chapter Seven

NANCY STARED AT him. "The murderer's after you?" she repeated. "How can you be sure?"

"Because there have been attempts on my life before! That was no heart attack I had. I was—"

Suddenly the door to his office burst open, and Paul Slesak stalked inside. "What kind of security do you have here?" he demanded. "Accident after accident! None of them should have happened!"

DuPres's cheeks flushed. "I agree with you. Since I was not here when the accidents occurred, I was hardly in a position to—"

"That is no excuse." Slesak swept his arguments away with a dramatic gesture. "Trent's death could have been avoided if there had been adequate maintenance and security. Which reminds me: someone has gone through my private recipes! Someone is trying to steal them. There is no security around this place! And if so much as one of my recipes is missing, I'll hold you personally responsible!"

"Get out of my office!" DuPres shouted, leaping to his feet. "You are no longer in charge. And I suggest you remember that!"

Slesak's look was murderous. He turned on his heel and stalked out, slamming the door until it shook in its casing.

Slesak was so angry he hadn't seemed to notice Nancy. Either that, or he had ignored her.

DuPres muttered a few words in French, high spots of color on his cheeks. Shaking his finger at the door, DuPres said, "I take back what I said. Paul Slesak could want me dead! He could! He wants this school for himself!"

"Enough to kill for it?" Nancy asked softly, waiting for DuPres to calm down.

"Maybe," he muttered, sinking slowly back into his seat. "Maybe."

"Let's go back to where we were before Chef Slesak interrupted," Nancy suggested. "You said the murderer must have made a mistake."

"That is correct."

"Well, that may be," Nancy said, treading

carefully. "But you and Chef Richards don't look anything alike. It seems more likely that whoever killed Richards did it on purpose."

DuPres leaned back in his chair, his face tired and pale. "The reason I say the killers were after me is because I did not have a heart attack. I was poisoned. The police have not leaked this to the press at my request. I did not want the reputation of the school jeopardized."

A chill ran down Nancy's spine. She'd been right all along. "Do the police have any clues?"

"Not yet. But I will make sure they put Chef Slesak on the top of their list of suspects!"

"Will you tell me about the threats you received?" Nancy asked.

DuPres took a deep breath. "Just before the poisoning I received a message—a message I could not mistake. It was a note with a skull and crossbones on it."

"Where is it now?" Nancy asked.

"It is missing. Someone took it from my chef's jacket sometime after I collapsed."

That could have been easy for Paul Slesak to engineer, Nancy thought grimly, but she kept her thoughts to herself.

"But that is not all," Chef DuPres went on. "A few weeks ago I was nearly run down by a delivery van here at the school. At first I thought it was an accident, but now I am sure it was not. The van could have easily avoided me."

"What kind of van was it?"

"It was unmarked. Gray. All I saw as it sped away was a broken taillight."

"Well, that's something to go on at least," Nancy murmured.

"I have told you these things only because you persisted, but you must not involve yourself any further, Ms. Drew." Chef DuPres frowned. "It is too dangerous."

"I'll watch my step," Nancy assured him. "But I can't give up the investigation now that I have something to go on." There was nothing more Nancy could say. Thanking DuPres for confiding in her, she walked out of his office.

Could Paul Slesak have murdered Trent Richards? she asked herself. Why? What, if anything, was the connection between the two men? It was more likely by far that Slesak was after DuPres. The pastry chef hadn't exactly kept it a secret that he was interested in running the school.

But DuPres's theory that the murderer had simply made a mistake didn't wash.

Nancy heaved a sigh of relief when her cooking class finally ended for that day. She needed to talk to Ned without fear of someone—such as Jacques Bonet—overhearing.

"We had a powwow at lunch," Ned told her as they walked back to the hotel. "George and I outvoted Bess and decided on pizza for dinner."

"What did Bess want?" Nancy squinted as she

looked up at him. Even this late in the afternoon the sun was still beastly.

"French food," Ned said with a grimace. "Your friend Bonet really made an impression on her."

"He's not just *my* friend," she said, digging through her purse for her sunglasses. "You know him as well as I do. Oh, no— I've lost my sunglasses. They were on my head in DuPres's office, but they must have slipped off."

Nancy glanced back. They were over halfway to the hotel. She was too hot and tired to go back for them.

"Tell you what," Ned said. "Let's go to the hotel and have a swim. We'll pick up your sunglasses on the way to get pizza."

"Good idea," Nancy said.

After a cooling swim and a nap on the sun deck, Nancy felt a thousand times better. When George and Ned said they were ready to get the pizza, she declined a ride. "I feel like walking," she said. "How about you, Bess? Want to come along?"

Bess lifted her own sunglasses to the top of her head, grimacing at her sun-pinkened skin. "Sure, why not?"

Dusk was falling as the two girls walked down the pathway to the school. "I'll wait in the main building," Bess said. "I'd like to talk to Chef Slesak for a minute."

"Be careful," Nancy warned. "Chef DuPres doesn't trust him."

Nancy crossed to DuPres's office building and climbed the stairs to the second floor. She tried his door, but it was locked tight.

When she returned to the main building, Bess wasn't outside waiting. "Hurry up, Bess," Nancy muttered, then tried the door to the school. Locked.

Nancy began walking slowly back to the hotel. George and Ned were undoubtedly back with the pizza. But where was Bess?

Evening shadows were lengthening near the towering laurel hedge along the walkway. Was that something moving ahead of her? Nancy stopped, squinting into the gathering darkness.

"Bess?" she called. "Are you there?"

The only answer was the rustle of leaves. In spite of the heat Nancy shivered.

She picked up her pace, circumventing the laurel hedge, crossing the street, and pausing under the light cast by the hotel's outdoor lamps.

Then, from a distance, Nancy heard, "N-a-a-a-ancy! Wait up!"

It was Bess! Straining her eyes, Nancy caught sight of her friend. She was across the street.

Nancy waved, then hurried back to meet her friend. She caught up with her near the laurel bushes. "Bess! Where have you been? I thought you had gone back."

"Nancy!" Bess grabbed her arm. "I saw Paul Slesak go into the school, so I followed him!"

Nancy's pulse quickened. "What happened?"

"He unlocked the door to his office and went inside. I peeked in through the door window and saw him go to his desk and unlock a drawer. Then he pulled out a white folder and all of a sudden he got really upset."

"By what he found in the folder?" Nancy asked.

"I guess so. He slammed his fist on the desktop and started yelling. Half of it was in German. I could barely understand him."

"But you could understand some of it?"

"Yes. He was mad about his recipes, about not being able to trust anyone."

"He complained about his recipes to Claude DuPres earlier today," Nancy said.

Quickly Nancy glanced around. Was someone there? Watching them? "Bess, come on. Let's get back to the hotel."

Before they could move, a white-robed figure suddenly sprang from behind the laurel hedge. Bess screamed as the figure swooped down on her.

But the figure wasn't after Bess. It was after Nancy. As she moved forward it grabbed her in a viselike grip, pinning her arms to her sides.

It's a man! Nancy thought wildly, struggling

with all her might against his incredible strength to see his face. But it was covered by a stocking.

Just as Nancy opened her mouth to scream, his white-gloved hand reached up and closed around her throat, cutting off her air.

Her attacker was strangling her!

Chapter Eight

"NANCY!" BESS SHRIEKED, running toward her to try to save her.

Nancy felt a release of pressure as her assailant turned to deal Bess one stunning blow. It sent her friend reeling backward.

Nancy pried at her attacker's fingers, gulping air. She was nearly free! She twisted, loosening his grip, and bit down hard on his wrist. He howled in pain—but then his fingers found her neck again. Was he going to kill her on the spot?

No. He was starting to drag her away.

"Nancy!" Bess screamed again, struggling to her feet. She flung herself on the white-robed attacker, but he knocked her down easily.

Dimly, Nancy heard running footsteps somewhere behind her.

"Let her go!" a familiar voice shouted grimly, and Ned hurled himself straight at the assailant.

Nancy felt a hard thud—and then she was free. Gasping, she staggered to her feet, her hands at her throat. Ned and the assailant were locked together, rolling on the ground.

"Ned!" she screamed, but her voice was weak and scratchy. She had to help him! She searched for a weapon—and then, to her horror, she saw the assailant's hand grabbing a rock.

"No!" Nancy lunged forward just as the attacker smashed the rock against Ned's temple. Ned crumpled, and the white-robed man twisted away, scrambling to his feet and leaving Nancy clutching at his billowing cape.

Nancy took two steps after him, but knew she would never catch him.

"Oh, Ned," she murmured, turning back and bending over him.

His eyes fluttered open. He groaned, reaching for his head.

"Is he all right?" Bess asked tremulously, getting to her feet.

"I'm okay, I think," Ned said, sitting up. "What about you?"

"I'm fine—now. Thanks to you."

Ned drew a deep breath and let it out again. "Who was that guy?"

"I don't know. I never saw his face. But he was in a chef's outfit, and he had on some kind of white robe."

Ned just looked at her. "A chef's outfit? This gets crazier by the minute. What was he trying to do to you?"

"I don't know, but it's clear somebody doesn't want me snooping around. How did you manage to rescue me just at the right moment?"

"When you didn't come back I got worried. I told George to stay at the hotel, and then I came looking for you." He stood up, swaying a bit.

Nancy put her arm around his waist. "Maybe you should lean on me," she suggested.

"Oh!" Bess suddenly exclaimed. "What if that guy was—"

"Shhh!" Nancy said. "Let's not talk here." With her arm firmly clasped around Ned's waist, she urged him in the direction of the hotel.

When they entered the lobby, they found George waiting anxiously. "What *happened* to you guys?" she asked. She was stunned when they recounted their story.

"He was so fast I couldn't even use judo on him," Nancy finished. She glanced anxiously once more at Ned's bump. "You sure you're all right?"

"I'm just hungry," he told her.

"Then you guys go down and sit in the rec room, and I'll bring the pizza," George said.

Nancy, Ned, and Bess found an empty card table. When they'd sat down, they realized that everyone was staring at them.

"I guess we look pretty bad, huh?" Bess remarked, wincing as she combed her blond hair with her fingers.

"Pretty bad," Ned agreed. "How's the throat?" he asked Nancy as George reappeared with the pizza.

"Okay," Nancy said, taking a slice. "But whoever attacked me wasn't kidding around."

Ned frowned. "This case is becoming dangerous."

"So what's the next move?" George asked Nancy.

Nancy picked up a Ping-Pong paddle and twirled it around in her hand. "Why was that guy wearing a chef's jacket?" Nancy asked. "It's a dead giveaway that he's associated with the cooking school."

"Paul Slesak," George stated with certainty.

Nancy shook her head. "It could have been, but we have no proof." Her expression grew thoughtful. "Someone must have overheard me talking to Chef DuPres. Or else he overheard my conversation with Bess. Why else would he feel threatened by me?"

"Didn't you say Slesak interrupted your meeting?" George said.

"He saw me there," Nancy agreed. "He could have been listening at the door."

Ned had been noticeably quiet. Now he spoke up. "I don't suppose you could blame this on Jacques Bonet?"

"Oh, you!" Bess threw a Ping-Pong ball at him. "It's no crime to be devastatingly handsome."

Ned made a gagging sound, and Nancy had to laugh. "Jacques doesn't seem to fit into the scheme of things," she said. "He said himself that he doesn't want to run the cooking school. He likes traveling around to different places."

"Maybe there's something else going on," Ned suggested.

Nancy nodded. "Trent Richards has to fit in somewhere. Bess, you still keep your eye on Paul Slesak, okay? But watch your step. He might be dangerous. I'll try to find out more from Claude DuPres and Jacques Bonet."

Ned held up his hand. "Whoa. Where does that leave me? *I'll* take care of Bonet."

"Okay." Nancy smiled. "But remember, he's not a criminal—so far as we know."

"So far as we know," Ned repeated, his voice distinctly chilly. "So far as we know."

On the way to class the following morning Nancy squeezed Ned's hand. "Cover for me, will you?" she said. "I'm going to try to see Claude DuPres again and pick up my sunglasses."

"Knowing how Bonet feels about you, he'll

probably send out the National Guard," Ned grumbled, but he split off from Nancy anyway.

Nancy was walking along, trying to decide how to gain more of Claude DuPres's confidence, when a headline from a newspaper vending machine caught her eye: COOKING SCHOOL ACCIDENT WARRANTS INVESTIGATION.

Quickly Nancy deposited a quarter and pulled out the top copy. She scanned the story. The article was full of innuendo, but no real facts. "Sources close to the school's head chef, Claude DuPres, suggest that DuPres may be an ineffectual manager," Nancy read. "Chef DuPres has also been accused of misappropriating funds needed to maintain the school and upgrade security . . ."

Nancy blinked. Hadn't she just heard nearly those exact words somewhere? She turned back to the article.

"The board of directors is calling an emergency meeting to determine whether or not Chef DuPres should resign."

Poor Claude DuPres, Nancy thought as she headed up to his office. It seemed so unfair.

Outside DuPres's office Nancy ran headlong into a group of reporters. They rushed up to her, notebooks in hand.

"Are you a member of DuPres's staff?" one asked her.

"No," Nancy murmured, taken aback. She knocked on the door, but wasn't surprised when there was no answer. She couldn't blame DuPres. The reporters were out for blood!

Ignoring them, she twisted the knob. When it turned in her hand, she had to hide her surprise.

DuPres was at his desk—on the telephone. When he saw Nancy, he nearly leapt from his chair. "I will have to call you back," he said coldly.

Nancy caught a glimpse of the same newspaper article she'd just read spread across his desk.

"Get out! Get out of here!" DuPres thundered after slamming down his phone. "You are responsible for this!" He bunched the newspaper in his fists and threw it across the room at her.

"What are you talking about? I couldn't have—"

"Get out!" DuPres slammed back his chair and strode over to her. His face was so red she was afraid he was going to burst a blood vessel.

"You!" he shouted, shaking his finger threateningly in front of her nose. "I want you off the premises and out of my school! If you do not leave this minute, I will throw you out myself!"

Chapter Nine

NANCY WAS DUMBFOUNDED. "I—I—" she began.

"The press is hounding me. My career is finished! And it is your fault. Your meddling has ruined me!" DuPres shouted.

"But the story in the newspaper has nothing to do with me," Nancy managed to say. "I couldn't know those things about the board of directors."

"Then who was the source? *Who?"*

Nancy shook her head. The pastry chef's name was on the tip of Nancy's tongue. It would be so easy to shift the blame to Slesak. But Claude

DuPres was so outraged that she decided against bringing up his name. "Maybe you need to look closer to home," she said instead. "Someone obviously knows a great deal about you and is using it to his advantage."

DuPres's jaw tightened. "This has ruined me!"

Nancy opened her mouth to ask more, but she was interrupted by a knock on the door. Before either of them could move, Jacques Bonet squeezed past the reporters and let himself inside.

"Jacques!" Claude greeted him in obvious relief.

"What's going on?" Jacques asked.

"Ask her," Claude said, pointing dramatically at Nancy. "She is meddling in my affairs."

Nancy's heart sank. He was too overwrought to listen to reason. "Chef DuPres feels I am somehow responsible for the newspaper article," she explained.

"What newspaper article?"

"You have not seen it?" DuPres gestured toward the floor where the crumpled newspaper lay. "There! See for yourself!"

Bonet picked up the newspaper and smoothed it out, his expression darkening as he read through the article. "Who can have done this?" he demanded, shaking the paper in his fist.

DuPres didn't answer, but his gaze was directed at Nancy.

"Nancy?" Jacques asked, surprised. "How

could Nancy have anything to do with this?"

Claude tossed up his hands. "She is asking questions all the time."

"Claude, there's no way Nancy could have spread these rumors even if she had a reason to."

For the first time Chef DuPres seemed to calm down. Nancy darted a grateful glance in Jacques's direction. It was clear Claude valued what the younger man said, and she was glad he was there to defend her.

"Who, then? Who would do this to me?" DuPres asked, bewildered. A moment later he answered his own question. "Paul Slesak! He has been after my position since he came here!"

He lapsed into an angry silence. Nancy broke it by asking whether he knew where her sunglasses were. DuPres handed them to her. Now he looked almost apologetic.

"Do you still want me to leave the school?" Nancy asked.

DuPres waved dismissively. "No, no. I am sorry. It cannot be your fault." He sighed. "But I am no longer doing the Washington dinner."

"What?" Jacques seemed to have turned to stone. "But it's only a few days away."

"It is true. They say I am a security risk. I am to be replaced."

"I don't believe it," Jacques muttered.

"Do not worry. They will keep you on. They need you."

"It's not me I'm worried about," Jacques retorted. "It's you. This is so unfair!"

"What is this Washington dinner?" Nancy asked.

Both men turned to her, blinking. She realized they'd forgotten she was listening. "Claude and I were to be head chefs at an important dinner for foreign dignitaries in Washington," Jacques said reluctantly. "It isn't for public record."

"And you've been replaced because of the newspaper article?" Nancy asked DuPres.

He narrowed his eyes at the younger chef and said, "I will make sure you are put in charge, Jacques. You are the most qualified."

Jacques clasped his friend's hand and said, "Let me know what I can do to help." Then he held the door for Nancy. "Time for class," he said.

The mass of reporters had dwindled to only a few. Jacques easily deflected them as he and Nancy headed down the stairs.

"Thanks for sticking up for me," she told him.

He shrugged. "Claude would have realized you couldn't have been the source soon enough. He just gets excited sometimes. Who do *you* think the source is?"

"I don't have any proof, but I'd bet on Paul Slesak."

"Slesak! Why?"

Nancy still wasn't sure she should tell him all

she knew. "It's just that DuPres and Slesak seem to be at each other's throats," she said.

"And you think that in itself would cause Slesak to make those damaging comments?"

"Yes. If he wanted the school for himself."

"Do you have any other theories?"

Nancy shook her head. She'd said more than she had intended to already. "All I've got on my mind today is cooking," she said brightly.

But cooking was definitely *not* what was on Nancy's mind that day. She wanted to concentrate all her energy on the mystery, and the hours she had to spend in class made her impatient.

When class ended Nancy and the others headed for the pool. Nancy swam several laps, working off some of her frustration as she considered her next move. Finally she pulled herself out of the water and flopped down on a lounge chair to tell the others what had happened in DuPres's office that morning.

"Hmmm. Did you notice how distracted Jacques seemed in class today?" Ned pointed out. "I wonder if it had anything to do with that Washington dinner thing?"

"Maybe." Nancy wrinkled her nose. "Although—aside from the fact that he was mad about the way DuPres was being treated—he didn't seem particularly displeased about taking over."

"All this talk about dinner is making me

hungry," Bess said. "What does everybody want to do about food?"

"Let's get some sandwiches from the coffee shop and eat outside," Nancy said.

"Best idea I've heard all day," Bess muttered.

Later that night as Nancy lay in bed, she struggled to come up with some answers. She felt as if her brain were locked up tight. I'm missing something important, she thought unhappily.

The next morning Nancy had to drag herself out of bed. Yawning, she padded to the bathroom to stare at her bleary-eyed reflection. "What should I do first?" she asked herself.

Paul Slesak, she thought. How should she begin investigating him? Suddenly it occurred to her that she hadn't been paying enough attention to one thing—Slesak's paranoia over his recipes. A feeling of excitement spread through her. His recipes! Of course. There had to be some reason he was so protective of them! She'd have to take a look at those recipes herself.

"What have you got cooking?" Ned asked when class was almost over that day.

Nancy was washing out her pan. "What do you mean?"

"In your *head,* Nancy. Not in your skillet."

Glancing around, Nancy leaned closer to Ned. "Remember how Slesak reacted when he found his recipes were missing? Well, I'm going to have a look at those recipes myself right after class."

"Not without me, you're not."

"I'd rather go alone," Nancy said. "It would look less suspicious if I got caught."

"I don't know . . ."

"Besides"—Nancy's eyes twinkled—"too many cooks spoil the broth. What I need you to do is follow Slesak. That way you can warn me if he starts getting too close."

"I still don't like it."

"Trust me," Nancy said, and Ned grudgingly gave in.

As soon as class was over, Nancy and Ned walked toward Paul Slesak's office. They saw the pastry chef just locking up, and hid out of sight until Slesak pushed through the exit doors.

"I'm on my way," Ned said, sauntering after him. "Be careful."

"Careful's my middle name," Nancy whispered after him, then tucked herself into a recessed doorway to wait until the halls had emptied. She didn't expect to hang around more than a few minutes, but when she kept hearing voices from inside the classrooms, she realized that some of the students were staying late to finish projects.

"Great," she muttered.

Finally the rooms were clear and the halls were empty. Nancy threw a glance outside. Night had fallen, and the hallways were slightly darkened, only every other light left on. The halls were utterly quiet.

Creeping to Paul Slesak's office door, she pulled her lock-picking set out of her purse. She slipped the pick inside the lock, her pulse accelerating. If she got caught now . . .

Was that a noise? Nancy glanced around. Not a whisper of air moved. Rapidly she twisted the pick in the lock. With a soft click the lock suddenly released, and the door swung inward.

Slesak's desk was in the center of the room. Nancy didn't waste any time. With painstaking care she worked the lock on the top drawer, glancing up every few seconds to make certain no one was coming. Finally the lock turned and Nancy pulled out the drawer. It was empty.

Feeling time race by, Nancy set about unlocking the next drawer. Her palms were wet, and she had to stop and wipe them on her jeans. Then the tumblers turned, and she slid the drawer open.

Inside was the white folder.

"Hallelujah!" Nancy murmured under her breath. Flicking on her penlight, she skimmed through the file.

Pastry recipe followed pastry recipe, from Bavarian creams to double-chocolate tortes. Everything looked delicious—but nothing looked unusual.

So what was the big deal?

Wishing she'd brought her pocket camera to

take pictures, Nancy slipped the recipes back in the folder, then laid them in the desk drawer. Gently she closed the drawer.

Slesak might just be secretive about his special recipes. Or paranoid. Or both. Nancy glanced at her watch again. She had to get out of there. Yet something about the recipes bothered her. What?

Suddenly Nancy heard soft footsteps outside the door. Frozen, she held her breath. Go on by, she pleaded silently. Just go right on by.

The door opened, and a man's hand reached inside to flip on the light. The room became bright. Nancy stood stock-still.

She was caught!

Chapter Ten

NANCY STOOD IN numb horror by Paul Slesak's desk. Her mind was racing, but she couldn't think of one excuse for being in the office.

The door swung silently inward, and there stood Jacques Bonet.

Nancy's shoulders slumped in relief. "Jacques," she said.

"What are you doing in here?" he asked.

"I was—well—" Nancy took a deep breath. "I was looking for Bess's wallet," she improvised. "She left it in the classroom, and I told her I'd come back to look for it."

Bonet's mouth curved. "An excuse to do a little spying?"

Nancy blushed. "Actually I'd hoped to run into Chef Slesak," she lied. "I wanted to ask him some questions."

Jacques consulted his watch. "I'm looking for him too. I thought he was going to be working late tonight."

Nancy's heart nearly stopped. What if Slesak had found her first? Was Ned still following him, or had he given up by now?

"Speaking of late, would you look at the time?" Nancy said in mock surprise. "I've got to get out of here."

"How did you get *in* here? The security guard locks the doors at night."

"Oh, I've been here awhile. Listen, I've got to get back, Jacques. I haven't had dinner yet, and I'm starved."

"What a coincidence. I haven't eaten yet either." Jacques regarded her thoughtfully. "Have dinner with me and I won't tell Paul I caught you in his office."

"I think that's blackmail."

He shrugged and smiled. "Whatever works. I still haven't had a chance to take you to Très Bon."

Nancy wasn't sure what to do. Still, the evening might not be a total waste if she played her cards right. "Okay, give me twenty minutes to get ready," she finally said.

"Done," Jacques said, and they walked out to his expensive-looking sports car.

Ned was going to hit the roof, Nancy thought glumly to herself. How would she be able to explain this date to him?

As Nancy was finishing dressing, the connecting door to George and Bess's room opened.

"Nancy!" George said. "Where have you been? And where are you going?"

"Jacques caught me in Paul Slesak's office, and I had to lie my way out of it. He told me that if I had dinner with him, he wouldn't tell Slesak I'd been in his office." Nancy sighed. "I just couldn't say no."

George shook her head. "I don't like that guy. What about Ned?"

"Ned doesn't know. But I'll call his room."

Nancy dialed swiftly, but there was no answer—and no time to find Ned. "I wish I knew where he was."

"Probably looking for you," George said darkly.

Nancy winced. "I asked him to follow Paul Slesak. You don't think he got into any trouble, do you?"

"Look, I saw Ned earlier for a second. He was fine, but he was worried about you. Go on your date. I'll handle it on this end. Just be careful, okay?"

Nancy kept looking for some sign of Ned as

she walked through the lobby, but he was nowhere. Jacques was waiting outside the door. He winked and waved when he saw Nancy, then held the car door for her as she climbed inside.

He didn't waste any time getting to the restaurant. The car sped like a bullet through the crowded city traffic.

Très Bon was an elegant restaurant done in mauve and gold. The sweeping crystal chandeliers were so huge they seemed to cover the ceiling. The maître d' led them to their table—an intimate place for two tucked into an alcove.

Jacques ordered for both of them. And Nancy tried her best to do justice to the food.

Well, she thought to herself, as long as I'm stuck here I might as well make the most of it. "When we were in Chef DuPres's office, you mentioned that this Washington dinner was kind of hush-hush," she said tentatively.

"Did I?" Jacques's smile didn't quite match his eyes.

"You must have special clearance even to be the chef at a dinner such as that."

Jacques regarded Nancy with faint amusement. "Why do I get the feeling you accepted my dinner invitation just to pump me for information?" he asked.

Nancy managed to hang onto her poise. "Sorry. Just a bad habit of mine, I guess."

She was glad when the check was paid and the

valet was retrieving the car. But when she felt Jacques's fingers smooth lightly over her bare arm, she had to force herself not to jerk away.

When they arrived back at the hotel, Nancy said, "Thanks a lot for dinner," and backed off as fast as she could toward the south wing.

At the elevator she heard a familiar voice call, "Hey." A very sober Ned walked toward her.

"Don't be mad," Nancy said before he could speak. "Please. I really didn't know how to get out of it."

"What about a simple no?"

"Well, you'll be happy to know the evening was a total waste. I didn't learn anything new," Nancy admitted.

"I did."

The elevator doors whisked open at that moment, but neither Ned nor Nancy stepped inside. "What do you mean?" Nancy asked.

Ned grabbed her arm and led her outside to the moonlit night. "I followed Slesak. He met with another man, someone I've never seen before. But there was something really secretive about him. He kept looking around, as if he was afraid someone was watching him. He and Slesak climbed into a car together," Ned added. "I ran back to my car and tore off after them, but I couldn't find them."

"I wonder who he is," Nancy murmured.

Ned exhaled heavily and draped his arm over Nancy's shoulders, giving her a hug. "Then I ran into George, and she told me you were having dinner with Bonet."

Nancy bit her lip. "Please don't be mad."

"I'm not mad, but I was worried. Nancy, I think Bonet's dangerous."

Nancy remembered the way Bonet had hustled her out of Paul Slesak's office. Had he wanted to make certain she wouldn't go back there? "Maybe he asked me to dinner just to keep an eye on me," she said, thinking about the evening.

"And now we will have Ms. Drew demonstrate her chicken cordon bleu," Jacques said the next day at the end of class.

Nancy was taken by surprise. Why was he choosing her? Her chicken wasn't anything special; in fact, it was a little dried out.

"I think it might have gotten a little overdone," she said apologetically, walking to the front of the room.

"Let me see. Put it on the counter here." Jacques indicated a space on the work island.

He stepped back, bumping the wrought-iron pot rack, which swung lazily from side to side. Nancy glanced up at it. She didn't remember the hook from which it hung being so exposed before.

Carefully setting her dish on the counter, Nancy said, "I really think mine's overcooked."

The wrought-iron rack above her head was still swaying a little, and it made her nervous. Glancing up, she said, "Is this thing safe? I don't remember it—"

She never finished her sentence. There was a sudden, terrible screech from above.

Nancy's heart seemed to stop beating. With a last wrench the rack tore loose from the ceiling and plummeted straight for her head!

Chapter Eleven

NANCY DIVED OUT of the way, hitting the floor just as the heavy rack crashed against the counter. Tiles splintered, and pans flew everywhere. Somebody screamed. Then a huge iron skillet slammed into Nancy's arm, numbing it from shoulder to elbow.

"Nancy!" Ned's voice was full of horror. He bent over her, his hands trembling when they touched her.

Jacques Bonet was also kneeling beside her. "Are you all right?" he asked anxiously.

"Nancy, don't move," Ned said. "I'll call an ambulance."

"No, I—think I'm okay." Nancy's voice was shaky. She cleared her throat, testing every muscle as she slowly sat up. Only her arm throbbed. "Really. I'm okay."

Nancy tested her arm. "It's not broken," she said with relief. "But I'm going to have one doozy of a bruise."

"I am canceling class for the rest of the day," Jacques said. Then he turned to Nancy. "Could I talk to you a moment?" His face was dark and set.

"Sure."

As soon as the last student had passed through the door, Jacques said, "Nancy, I haven't been totally honest with you. I think I know why these accidents have been happening."

"Why?"

He opened his mouth, then closed it again, as if he was reluctant to speak his mind. Finally he sighed and said, "I think the accidents are Claude's fault."

Nancy blinked. "Claude's fault? How can that be?"

"I didn't want to believe it. I still don't. But it's the only thing that makes sense."

"It doesn't make sense to me," Ned put in.

Bonet ignored him. "Claude's reputation as a chef has been declining in recent years. He's slowly losing his edge. To be truthful, I've been covering for his mistakes whenever I could."

There was silence for a moment. "But why would Claude sabotage his own school?" Nancy asked.

"To satisfy a wounded ego?" Jacques suggested.

"I can't believe that. He was horrified at the bad publicity. He even blamed me," Nancy reminded him.

Jacques expression was pained. "He's blamed me for things beyond my control as well. He hinted that I had engineered the loss of the Washington dinner."

"Oh, no."

"If these accidents don't stop, someone else will either be hurt or killed. What do you suggest we do, Nancy?" Jacques asked.

Nancy shook her head. She couldn't really believe what Jacques was saying. Claude DuPres was still a world-renowned chef. Although he was excitable, he hardly seemed like an egomaniac—certainly not in the way Jacques described him. But who knew DuPres better than Jacques? No one.

"Paul Slesak still has a stronger motive," Nancy argued. "If the accidents at the school make the board of directors lose faith in Claude DuPres, it paves the way for Slesak to take over."

"Claude would never stand for it," Jacques said. "And Paul knows that."

The coldness of Jacques's tone led Nancy to believe he was no fan of Paul Slesak's, either. "None of this makes sense," she said with a sigh. "And none of it seems a strong enough motive for murder."

"Who's talking about murder?" Jacques demanded.

Ned took a step forward to stand right next to Nancy. "Nancy and I don't believe Trent Richards's death was an accident. We think someone killed him."

"You obviously haven't read today's paper then," Jacques retorted. "The coroner's office says he slipped, hit his head, and then froze to death. It was definitely an accident. The police don't suspect foul play. Why should you?"

"We don't know *what* the police suspect yet." Nancy was doing her best to remain patient. "The coroner's report was just a preliminary."

Jacques shook his head. "*Why* would anyone want Trent Richards dead?"

"That," Nancy answered grimly, "is what this mystery is all about."

She and Ned left Bonet in the classroom and headed back to the hotel, where Nancy spent a frustrating afternoon trying to learn more from the police department about Trent Richards's death. At four-thirty she announced to Ned, "I've gone about this all wrong. The person I really need to face is Paul Slesak."

"Oh, no." Ned was adamant. "Not without me."

Nancy smiled. "I was hoping you'd say that."

When they looked in Slesak's classroom and office, the pastry chef wasn't around. "Where could he be?" Nancy asked Ned.

"Maybe he left for the day."

"It's a little early for him to end his class, isn't it? I guess I'll just camp outside his door and wait."

"Until tomorrow?"

"No, silly, but for a few hours anyway. If he hasn't come back by, say, six-thirty, I'll leave."

"I'll keep you company," Ned said.

While they waited, Ned asked, "So what do you think of Bonet's theories about DuPres?"

"I don't know. They seem farfetched, don't they?"

Ned agreed. "But why would Bonet finger his friend if he really didn't believe it?"

"Beats me."

When the school had all but emptied, Nancy said, "I don't think Slesak's coming back. But before we leave, let's have a look around the school."

Downstairs Ned put his finger to his lips at the sound of voices. "They're not coming from the freezer, are they?"

Nancy shook her head. "No, I think they're in

the butchering room across from it. And one of them sounds like Slesak!"

They ran down the hall and stopped in front of the butchering room. Through the small window in the door they could see both Slesak and DuPres.

"You will get what you deserve," Slesak spat out. "The board will make their decision."

DuPres's face was flushed with anger. "The board will see you for the fake you are!" he volleyed back.

"You insult me for the last time!" Slesak roared and grabbed a cleaver, brandishing it in front of DuPres's face. His eyes glittered dangerously.

"Chef Slesak—" Nancy shouted, yanking the door open. But neither man paid any attention to her.

DuPres swept up a wicked-looking butcher knife. "We will decide this here and now!" DuPres yelled. As Nancy looked on in horror, he swung his knife at Slesak's head!

Chapter Twelve

"STOP!" NANCY SCREAMED. She rushed forward and grabbed hold of Slesak, pulling him back. Her hand wrapped around his wrist until the cleaver clattered to the floor.

"Get back, Nancy!" Ned yelled.

DuPres's face was dangerously flushed. He took another step toward Slesak, his weapon held high.

"He is a crazy man!" Slesak sputtered. "He tried to kill me!"

"That's not the whole story, pal," Ned said,

grabbing DuPres by the shoulder. "We saw you pick up the cleaver first."

Suddenly DuPres's arm dropped as if the knife had grown too heavy. Nancy dropped Slesak's arm and walked up to the other man. DuPres looked totally defeated. He wiped a trembling hand across his face.

"What's going on?" a voice said from the doorway.

Nancy turned. "Jacques!" she said.

Bonet's gray eyes sized up the situation in a glance. He walked straight to Claude DuPres and put a supportive arm around him.

"He was searching my office. He tried to kill me," Slesak said in a surly voice. "He is not fit to run this school!"

"I was looking for you!" DuPres shouted with a momentary return of spirit. "You followed me here to attack me!"

"Hah!" Slesak spat disdainfully and stalked out, slamming the door behind him.

Jacques regarded Claude soberly. "What was that all about—really?"

DuPres sighed. "Slesak did not tell the truth. I came to his office to find him. He was not there, so I went to the freezer to make certain the door is working again. And then I came here."

"Why did you come here?" Nancy asked.

"To make certain everything was safe."

Jacques's eyes met Nancy's over the top of

DuPres's head. "You look tired, Claude. Let me drive you home," Jacques said.

"I would appreciate that," DuPres said formally.

By unspoken agreement Nancy, Ned, and Jacques walked the older chef outside. "I'll be back with my car," Jacques said, and he took off toward the hotel.

Nancy and Ned lingered with DuPres.

"It is only a matter of time before the board replaces me," DuPres said quietly. "My health is failing. So is my reputation," he continued. "But I cannot bear the thought of Paul Slesak taking over my school."

"What about Jacques Bonet?" Ned asked. "He seems to have the right reputation."

"He is too young. And anyway, he is too restless. He wants much, much more than just one school."

Jacques's sports car pulled up, and Nancy watched as the younger chef helped the older one into the car. As the sports car made a tight U-turn and sped away, Nancy turned to Ned. "Let's not go back yet," she said. "I want to walk around awhile and do some thinking."

"All right."

They strolled down the pathway in silence. After a few minutes Nancy stopped short. "I've got an idea."

"What? No, don't tell me. Can it wait until after dinner?" Ned asked.

Nancy continued as though she hadn't heard him. "Do you think Slesak's left the school yet? We never really got a chance to talk to him."

"You want to go wait around his office *again?*"

"Just for a little while. Look, if you go with me, just for an hour or so, we'll go get burgers or pizza or take-out Chinese—whatever you want, my treat."

"Well, okay. But I'm watching the clock."

Slowly they went back into the building and returned to Paul Slesak's office. "The light's on," Nancy said. "Maybe he's here."

Ned grabbed her arm. "Yeah, but look who's coming!"

Nancy turned around and looked out the hall window. She could see Jacques Bonet's sports car wheeling into the school parking lot.

"Come on," Ned said. "Let's get out of sight."

They ran past Slesak's office and turned at the nearest branching corridor. As she pressed against the wall, Nancy could hear Jacques's determined footsteps pounding up the stairs.

She heard a door open, then softly shut. She peeked around the corner. "He must have gone into Slesak's office," she said excitedly.

She tiptoed down the hallway, then crouched in front of Slesak's door. Ned kept a lookout.

Paul Slesak was speaking, but Nancy could only catch about one word in ten. "Information . . . in the wrong hands. If maintenance—"

Bonet's answer was lost to her entirely. Then

Slesak suddenly shouted, "You had no right to steal the recipes!"

Nancy's lips parted. She wished she dared look through the window in the door.

"Psst," came a soft warning.

Nancy glanced at Ned and read his signals. Someone was coming! She straightened, looking around for somewhere to hide. There was no place. We'll have to bluff our way out, she realized as she tiptoed to where Ned was standing. "I can't find it," she said out loud, seeing a chef just a few feet from her. "I've looked everywhere, and I just can't find it! I guess I'll have to come back and try to find it tomorrow," Nancy said, heaving an exaggerated sigh. "Let's go."

Ned chuckled as they stepped into the warm evening air. "It's a good thing that chef didn't ask you *what* you were trying to find. Did you hear anything at Slesak's door?"

"Not much, but one thing may be important." She reported the pastry chef's words. "Why do you suppose Jacques stole Slesak's recipes?"

"Maybe he wants to take a shortcut to success, like Trent Richards. He figured he could use Slesak's recipes."

"But that doesn't make sense. Jacques already has an excellent reputation. And Claude DuPres made it clear he thinks Slesak is second-rate."

Ned shrugged. "Then you've got me."

Nancy took Ned's hand as they began walking back to the hotel. "What is the deal with those recipes?" she mused out loud. "I wish I'd gotten a better look at them."

"You said they were just recipes."

"They were. But there was something about them. . . . " She sighed. "I'll think about it tomorrow. For now, let's go take a swim."

They got back to the hotel and split up. "I'll meet you down here in ten minutes," Ned told her.

"Make it five," Nancy answered, smiling. She walked quickly to the south wing. There was no one around. As she approached the elevator, movement caught her eye. She looked up in time to see a man hurrying around the corner with some kind of wooden sign.

The elevator doors opened. Nancy stepped inside and rang for her floor. She leaned against the railing as the doors closed again.

But instead of making a smooth start, the elevator jerked. A dreadful clanking noise accompanied its progress upward. A sick feeling spread in the pit of her stomach. Something was terribly wrong.

At the fifteenth floor the car started to slow down. Heart pounding, Nancy squeezed her fingers between the doors, trying to wedge them open. Nothing happened.

Then the elevator jerked to a bouncing stop. Nancy pounded her fists against the doors. "Help!" she screamed. "Help me!"

The car shuddered once. Nancy pulled on the doors with all her might. Then something snapped, and the car plunged downward at dizzying speed. The elevator cable must have broken!

She was racing to her death at the bottom of a black abyss.

Chapter Thirteen

NANCY SCREAMED. THE lights were a blur outside the elevator window. With every second the car gathered momentum, plummeting toward the ground below.

I'm going to die, she thought, terror-stricken.

All of a sudden the lights went out—every light, inside and out. The elevator hurtled downward in total darkness.

Nancy closed her eyes. She was so scared she couldn't breathe. An eternity seemed to pass in a few seconds.

Then the car suddenly jerked. Nancy was

thrown to one side. She opened her eyes. Was it her imagination, or was the car starting to slow? Nancy dared not even move a muscle.

It *was* slowing! Nancy was so relieved she felt tears sting her eyes. Her mouth trembled as the elevator finally crawled to a shuddering stop. She didn't move. She was afraid—afraid the car would begin its downward plunge again.

She was still rooted to the spot when the doors slid open. The elevator hadn't stopped exactly at the first floor, Nancy realized. It was out of line, and Nancy was standing slightly above the small crowd of people who stood outside. Arms shaking, she jumped down just as Ned, Bess, and George raced forward.

"What's going on?" Ned demanded.

"I—I don't know." Nancy tumbled into his arms. "It just started falling."

"Where's the sign?" a man asked.

"What sign?" Ned looked at the man.

"The warning sign."

Nancy's mind suddenly flashed back. "I saw a man taking something, but I didn't know what it was. It must have been the sign.

"Someone's definitely trying to kill me," Nancy whispered to Ned.

He pulled her away from the crowd just as a maintenance man in blue coveralls appeared.

"Who used this elevator?" the maintenance man demanded.

"I did." Nancy took a deep breath.

"Can't you read?" the man demanded. "This thing's been out of order all day."

"There was no sign," Ned explained grimly. "Someone removed it."

The maintenance man turned pale.

"Why wasn't the elevator turned off?" George asked him.

"It was. Ever since it started jamming this morning. In fact, I'd turned off the operation switch and was checking it out. Then it suddenly broke loose." He inclined his head toward Nancy. "Your friend there wouldn't have survived if I hadn't been on top of things."

Nancy shuddered. "How could the elevator break loose if you'd thrown the operation switch?"

"That's what I don't understand. Someone had to turn it back on," he muttered. "But I'm the only one authorized to do it."

"Something's up," Nancy said. "And somebody thinks I'm getting too close. Let's get out of here."

"Who was the man who stole the sign?" Bess asked as they walked away.

"I don't know. But it wasn't Paul Slesak or Jacques Bonet. Neither of them could have made it back here from the cooking school in time."

"So who does that leave? DuPres?" George asked.

"No!" Nancy was adamant. "We saw Jacques take him home."

"We saw Jacques drive him out of the parking lot," Ned corrected her. "We don't know where he went after that."

"It's all connected somehow," Nancy muttered, her thoughts churning. She checked her watch. "I'm going back over to the school."

"Tonight?" Bess and George chorused.

"What better time? Bonet's office is there. If he's got Slesak's recipes, it's a good bet he's keeping them there."

"Then I'm coming with you," Ned said.

"Okay. I think I'd better bring my camera too."

"Bess and I will do our best to get into Bonet's room and search it," George said.

"What?" Bess stared at her cousin in dismay.

"Maybe we can get ourselves invited over." George ignored Bess's affronted look. "Flirting is your specialty, Bess. See if you can't wangle an invitation out of him."

Nancy checked her watch. "It's after nine. We're going to have to break into the school."

"You sure this is such a good idea?" Bess asked.

"I'd rather be at the school when no one's there. I'm going to go upstairs to change and get my camera. Ned, I'll meet you back here in ten minutes. Then we'll all rendezvous at midnight. If anyone fails to show, we'll know he or she's in trouble. Agreed?"

"Agreed," Bess answered first. "And if midnight comes, and someone's not back?"

"Then we'll have to assume they've been caught," Nancy said soberly.

"What time is it?" Ned asked half an hour later as they stood outside the school doors.

Nancy checked the illuminated dial on her wristwatch. "Just after ten. If we don't get in soon, we might as well forget it. We'll never get back in two hours."

They moved stealthily around the grounds, keeping close to the walls and being careful to stay out of sight of the floodlights. Testing windows and doors, they circled the entire building. There was no way in.

Nancy heaved a sigh, her gaze searching the building. "I can't see how—" She broke off. "Look! There's an open window on the second floor." She gauged the distance. "Huh-uh, we'll never be able to reach it."

Ned considered it carefully. "Well, I could boost you up, and you could open the door for me."

"Good. Let's just hope this place isn't wired with alarms."

Glancing around, Nancy kicked off her shoes, then accepted a leg up from Ned. She pushed against the pane, then grabbed the edge of the sill and hooked her elbows inside. With a boost from Ned she managed to haul herself over the sill and tumble with a clatter onto one of the classroom counters.

"Nancy!" Ned whispered from down below. "Are you okay?"

She stuck her head back outside and signaled in the direction of the door. Ned took off at a sprint.

Climbing down from the counter, Nancy moved as noiselessly as possible to the door. It opened with a soft creak—but to her it sounded like a screech. Looking both ways, she hurried barefoot to the stairs.

On the first floor she checked again. Ned was waiting outside the door. With an effort Nancy reached the upper dead bolt. Then she pulled back the bottom one. Pressing on the bar, she let Ned inside. No alarms sounded.

"Okay, here we go," Nancy said. She turned on her penlight.

They didn't speak as they found their way to Jacques's office. The door was locked, but Nancy easily picked her way inside.

"Lock the door behind us," she instructed Ned. "Just in case someone should come."

The office was sparsely decorated. Obviously Jacques didn't use it much. A can of paint and a roller stood in one corner. The scent of fresh paint still lingered in the air.

"There's hardly anywhere to look," Nancy said. "Let's search the desk."

The drawers were all unlocked. A brief examination revealed that there was nothing worth locking up inside.

Nancy's eyes swept over the bare office. Why had she thought there would be anything there? "But he should have *something* here," she murmured to herself. "His own recipes, for instance. His own personal supplies."

"He must have them in his hotel room. He wouldn't leave them in the classroom."

Ned walked over to the bookcase. It was built in, but only a few shelves held books. The rest were empty. Ned picked up one of the books and fanned through the pages. "Nothing here."

Nancy walked up to him, checking the books' titles. They were all cooking manuals. One had been written by Claude DuPres.

"Why can't we find out anything about Jacques?" she asked. "Other than his association with Chef DuPres, Jacques's background is a mystery."

"Will the real Jacques Bonet stand up?" Ned joked as he put the book back.

Nancy was eyeing the bookcase. "Ned, look," she said excitedly, pointing to one of the shelves. "The back panel is painted a slightly different color."

Nancy touched the panel. The paint still felt slightly sticky, as if it were new. "There's something here!" she whispered. "This panel's not like the others."

Searching with her hand, she felt all around

the shelf. All of a sudden the back panel slid sideways. It happened so quickly that Nancy blinked, hardly able to believe her luck.

"Is there anything inside?" Ned asked.

"I think so. Wait a minute." Nancy reached in and carefully withdrew a manila envelope. She opened the flap and slid out the contents of the envelope. Several papers fluttered to the ground. Nancy picked them up and scanned them quickly.

"They're recipes!" Nancy said in a rush. "The pastry recipes I saw in Chef Slesak's office!"

Ned exhaled. "And that means—"

"I know." Nancy met his gaze. "It means Jacques Bonet is a thief."

Chapter Fourteen

"Quick! Let's take some pictures," Nancy said. "There's got to be a reason Jacques took these from Slesak."

Nancy pulled out her miniature camera and snapped photo after photo.

When she was finished she slipped the recipes back in the envelope and stashed it back in the bookcase. By the time she checked her watch again, she realized she had almost used up her two hours.

As they hurried down the corridor to the door, Ned asked, "What about the dead bolts?"

Nancy couldn't wait to get out of the building, but she knew it would be a lot more prudent to wipe out any trace of their break-in. "I'll let you out, relock the dead bolts, then meet you at the window."

"Aye, aye."

Carefully Nancy entered the room she had broken into. She looked out the window and saw Ned in the shadows below. She climbed out the window, hanging precariously as she waited to feel Ned's hands on her heels.

"Who's there?" It was Paul Slesak! His voice echoed through the still night.

Ned's hands grasped Nancy's heels, and he gave her a quick jerk. She tumbled downward, clutching at air, but Ned caught her before she hit the ground.

Footsteps sounded on the concrete. "You there!" Slesak's voice rang out. "Stop!"

There was no way to escape. Slesak and a man Nancy didn't recognize suddenly appeared directly in front of them.

"So it's you, Ms. Drew. What are you doing here?" Slesak said stonily.

Nancy couldn't think of anything to say. "I was—we were—taking a walk."

"Here?" His eyes swept the flower beds and he noticed her bare feet.

"Well, it's silly, really," she said, stalling. "I'm even embarrassed to admit it." She giggled and looked shyly at Ned. "We were just chasing each other. My sandals are slip-ons, and they came off."

"That's right. We were just fooling around," Ned said sheepishly. "We didn't think anyone would mind."

Slesak looked as if he didn't know what to think. His companion, a heavyset man with a blank expression, said nothing.

"Good grief, it's after midnight!" Nancy exclaimed.

"After midnight!" Ned repeated. "Bess and George will kill us. We were supposed to meet them."

"We'd better get back. Bye, Mr. Slesak!" Quickly Nancy slipped into her sandals. She grabbed Ned's arm, and the two of them rushed away.

"Think they believed us?" Nancy panted.

"Not for a minute," Ned answered soberly. "But we threw them off balance for a while. Nancy, that guy with Slesak is the one he was talking to yesterday. Could he have been the one who took the elevator sign?"

"Maybe. I didn't see him clearly enough. But in any case let's get back to the hotel now!"

Bess and George were waiting for them in the main lobby. "What happened?" Bess asked. "We were getting worried."

"I'll tell you later," Nancy said. With a quick

kiss goodbye to Ned, she and the cousins went to the elevator.

"We couldn't get into Bonet's room," George said. "He was in there all night, talking on the telephone. We knocked once, and Bess asked him to join us in the rec room, but we could tell he wasn't interested."

Nancy told them about the pictures once they were inside her room. "Thank goodness it's Saturday tomorrow," she said. "No classes. As soon as the stores open I'm going to find a one-hour film processing place. I've got to figure out what these recipes are all about. And I've got to do it soon."

The mall was already crowded by the time Nancy, Ned, Bess, and George arrived.

"It usually only takes an hour," the processor at the quick-photo shop assured them. "But the machine broke down. I'm sorry."

"When will the pictures be ready?" Nancy asked.

"Probably late afternoon or early evening."

Nancy wanted to scream with frustration, but she managed a weak smile. "Okay," she said.

"Well, let's kill some time by eating," Ned said. "As I recall, you promised me Chinese food last night."

"All right, let's find a Chinese restaurant," Nancy said.

"Brown sauce with just a touch of chili oil," George pronounced an hour later, biting into the first dish of chicken and peanuts. "A little on the mild side for my taste."

"Are you kidding?" Bess fanned herself with her napkin.

"Bess," Nancy asked, "what do you think of Paul Slesak as a chef in general?"

"I don't know." Bess shrugged. "He seems to know what he's doing. Although I've learned not to ask too many questions."

"Why's that?"

"It always seems as though he's got bigger fish to fry," Bess went on. "I get the feeling he's just putting up with us."

"Like Trent Richards," Nancy said. "It sure seems as if the Claude DuPres International Cooking School is filled with chefs who want something more."

"They're all egomaniacs," Ned agreed.

"Except Jacques Bonet," Bess said.

Ned snorted. "*Especially* Jacques Bonet."

"No, Bess is right," Nancy said. "Jacques doesn't seem to be climbing the ladder to success. He's already made it."

"So why did he steal the recipes?" George asked.

They all looked at one another. "That," Nancy said determinedly, "is what I'm going to find out."

When they returned to the mall they checked

with the film processor. He told them it would still be a while, so they shopped.

It was nearly six o'clock before the pictures were finally ready. Unwilling to examine them in such a public place, Nancy waited until they were back at the hotel. Then she, Ned, Bess, and George met in Ned's room. They fanned the photos out on the floor and pored over them.

"They're just recipes," Bess declared disappointedly after they'd looked at them.

"It sure looks that way," Ned agreed.

"But they're written to feed an army." George lifted her palms in surrender. "You figure it out. I sure can't."

Ned lay on his back on the floor, holding a photo above his head. "Chocolate cake for seven hundred and fifty," he said wryly. "What a lot of butter."

"Let me see that again." Bess snatched the photo out of his grasp. "That's funny. The proportions are all wrong," she said after a minute.

"What do you mean?" Nancy reached for the photograph, and Bess placed it in her outstretched hand.

"That's not how you make chocolate cake. We made it in class. There are ingredients here that don't fit in. Ned's right—there is too much butter."

A feeling of excitement swept over Nancy.

"Twenty-nine pounds of salt," she murmured. "And only seven pounds of sugar. You don't suppose it's some kind of code, do you?"

"Code?" Ned took another look at the recipe over her shoulder. "What kind of code? Why would a pastry chef need a code?"

"Maybe Slesak's not just a pastry chef."

Bess, George, and Ned stared at Nancy as if she'd lost her mind. "Well, think about it," she said. "We already know that Claude DuPres thinks Slesak's a poor excuse for a chef."

"Well, what does that make him?" Bess asked.

"I'm not sure. But what if he's got some kind of information here that's really important? Maybe something stolen or classified."

"Why would he have it at a cooking school?" Ned asked skeptically. "And what do you suppose Jacques Bonet wanted with the recipes?"

"That's what—" Nancy started to say. "Someone's here!" She moved like lightning. "Quick. Grab the photos and hide them."

But before they could move, Ned's door swung inward so violently the wall shook.

"Hey!" Ned said angrily. "How did you—" He stopped short, his eyes staring down the nose of a blue snub-nosed revolver.

Holding Ned in his gunsights, Paul Slesak

stretched one arm out toward the pictures in Nancy's hands. "Thank you for retrieving my recipes for me. Now, hand them over," he said coldly. "Unless you want to say goodbye to your friend here"—his finger tightened on the trigger—"forever."

Chapter Fifteen

"TIE THEM UP!" Slesak called over his shoulder, and Slesak's mysterious friend from the night before lumbered into the room, closing the door behind him.

He snatched the photographs from Nancy's hand, yanked out a coil of tough, narrow rope from inside his jacket, and bound her hands so hard and fast that her fingers started to go numb instantly.

"Who are you?" she demanded. "What's going on?"

The heavyset man smiled as he tied up Bess

and George, showing off a pair of flat, even teeth. "We're just a couple of guys trying to make a living."

"Shut up, Colville!" Slesak commanded.

"What's with the recipes?" Nancy asked. "What kind of information have you got hidden there?"

Colville couldn't quite hide his surprise. His jaw slackened. But Slesak said, "You are grossly mistaken, Ms. Drew." He lowered his gun as Colville bound Ned's hands behind his back.

Nancy spoke up quickly, "I think not. I think there's more to these recipes than meets the eye. Why else would you want them so badly?" she asked.

"I am only taking what is rightfully mine," Slesak told her. "Look elsewhere for your thief."

"So you're the good guys, huh?" Ned asked. "How come I don't believe that?"

"Gag him," Slesak ordered Colville. "And the others too."

"What are you going to do with us?" Bess asked tremulously.

"I have not decided yet."

Nancy suddenly spied a manila envelope poking out from Slesak's jacket pocket. It was the envelope from Jacques's office. "You already stole them back!" she said.

"Now I have all the copies. And I am afraid your fate is sealed."

Slesak signaled with his gun. After checking

the hall, Colville shoved Nancy and her friends out the door. Nancy walked as slowly as she could. If only someone would come along!

"Hurry up," Slesak growled. Colville forced the four down the many flights of stairs and into the pitch-black night. Nancy dragged her feet, trying to buy time.

They skirted the main hotel and parking lot and were herded toward a narrow side street. A gray van with a broken taillight was parked on the corner. A van with a broken taillight? Nancy thought. Claude DuPres had nearly been run over by a van like that!

"Tie their feet," Slesak ordered, and Colville dumped each of them in the back and did as instructed. Just before the van door rattled closed, Nancy got a quick glimpse of a barren, closed-in rectangle.

Nancy scooted toward the front of the van where a wall separated the cab from the back. It was so dark that she couldn't make out anything. She struggled to sit upright. The engine fired, and the van trembled beneath her.

As the van picked up speed, Nancy became certain they were on a highway. The first thing to do was get rid of her bonds. She tried to remember if there was anything—some little hook or sharp-edged piece of metal—in the van. Her one glimpse hadn't been sufficient to show her.

The van turned off the highway and began twisting down another road. Traffic noise diminished. They were moving away from civilization! Nancy struggled even harder to loosen the rope around her wrists. Her mouth was as dry as sand.

She had been so involved with her escape that at first she didn't realize the dull hum coming through the wall of the van was conversation. Colville and Slesak were talking to each other.

Nancy pressed her ear to the wall. She could only make out snatches of their conversation.

"I'm worried about being found out," Colville said hotly. "These are just kids!"

"You knew the risks when you got into this." Slesak's voice was hard. "Shut up and drive."

Colville's voice lowered, and Nancy had to strain to catch just a few of his words. She thought she heard him say, "A double cross . . . not going to like it . . . Information worth millions to the right political party!"

Nancy's eyes widened. Political party? Slesak and Colville *were* involved in the transfer of classified information! *Stolen* classified information, no doubt. The pieces of the puzzle were finally beginning to fall into place!

What seemed like hours went by. Nancy was beginning to think they were driving across the entire state. Then there was a sudden surge of acceleration and the van leapt forward. It seemed to coast for a moment, then the engine sputtered and died.

Nancy expected the rear doors to open. She was surprised when nothing happened. Silence surrounded her. Then she heard a ripping sound. "I've got my gag off!" Ned said. "My hands are free. I worked the ropes loose."

His hands groped across her face, and he jerked off her gag. Nancy's tongue felt like dried leather. "Ned, they're selling political secrets! I heard Slesak say—" She broke off in a gasp as a gush of ice-cold water soaked her feet and legs. "What's that?"

"Water," Ned said tersely. He worked feverishly to untie her. Then they both rushed over to Bess and George. The van was starting to sway back and forth.

"It's freezing! We must be in a river or something!" Bess cried as soon as her gag was off.

The swaying motion continued. Nancy went cold inside. "We're sinking," she whispered to herself.

"We're trapped in here." George's voice drifted toward Nancy in the darkness. Nancy could hear the panic beneath her words.

"I'm going to kick the door open," Ned said through his teeth. "Get ready."

"We're not going to make it," Bess said fearfully. "We're all going to die."

"Shhh!" Nancy reprimanded her sharply. "We're going to be fine."

Ned kicked the door furiously. At first it didn't budge. Nancy bit her lip. If he didn't get it open, they had no chance. She could feel water swirling halfway up her calves.

Bam! With a final hard kick the doors flew open. A torrent of water burst inside. It was over their heads!

Nancy flailed her arms, gasping for air. The van was sinking, and they were all going down with it!

Chapter
Sixteen

NANCY TRIED TO call Ned, but water filled her throat. She coughed and choked. She lost her sandals as she kicked through the water. Her lungs were bursting. Her fingers clawed along the sides of the van. She would never get out. Never!

Then her head surfaced for just an instant. Water was bubbling and swirling inside the van. She saw Bess's blond head and tried to reach for her.

"Bess!" Nancy called, but Bess had sunk beneath the water. Of all of them, Bess was the weakest swimmer.

Nancy's hand suddenly connected with the edge of the van door. She heaved herself outside and kicked up. Her head broke water and she drew a huge breath.

"Nancy!" she heard someone call.

"George!" she cried. "Bess is in the van!"

"I've got Bess," George yelled. "I got her out!"

"Nancy!" This time it was Ned who called her name. "Are you okay?"

"Yes." She coughed again. Her arms ached. The shore seemed a long distance away.

Ned's head was bobbing several yards away. "I'm going to help George with Bess," he called. "Can you make it to shore?"

"No problem."

Nancy glanced at the shore. She treaded water, trying to conserve her energy. Taking a deep breath, she closed her eyes and stroked. Take it easy, she told herself. Don't hurry. Don't panic. She swam cleanly, wasting no effort. You can make it, she told herself over and over again.

Her arms were starting to give out, so she rolled over and floated on her back, staring up at the starlit sky. They were in a huge lake, she realized. A lake as big as a sea.

Turning over again, she pulled herself through the water. At last her toe touched gravel. She surfaced, coughing and sputtering. "I made it!" she shouted.

"Great!" Ned called back. "We'll be right there."

A bubbling over to her right was the last sign Nancy had of the sinking van. She thanked her lucky stars the air trapped inside the back of the van had kept it afloat as long as it had.

"Where are we?" George asked as she and Bess and Ned swam up to Nancy.

"Well—" Nancy made a face. "It's a big lake, and we drove a long way. I have no idea where we are."

Bess got to her feet. "Let's get going. Wherever we're going."

They struck off down the highway. Nancy had to bite her lip to keep from complaining about her bare feet. She was shivering even though the night was warm, and her clothes felt stiff and sticky.

"Need someone to keep you warm?" Ned asked, putting his arm around her.

"What I wouldn't do for a bike," Nancy answered.

"What I wouldn't do for a car," Bess moaned.

"What about some talk?" Ned asked. "Nancy, you said something about political secrets."

"I think Slesak's private recipes are actually a code for the transfer of political secrets."

"What?" George stared at her. "How do you figure that?"

"Slesak and Colville were talking about it. Colville was worried. He talked about getting money for their political secrets."

"Really?" Bess said. "What has that got to do with Slesak's wanting to run the cooking school?"

"I think it's his cover. After all, he *is* a chef. A cooking school would be a perfect cover."

"Where does Jacques Bonet fit into all of this?" George put in. "I mean, why did he steal the recipes from Slesak? He must have known what was going on."

"Yes, he must have," Nancy agreed quietly. "I'll have to figure out what he's up to."

It was nearly dawn before they found their way to a major highway. "Civilization!" Ned shouted when headlights finally came toward them. He waved frantically, and Nancy, Bess, and George did the same.

The car slowed down and stopped. The woman on the passenger's side rolled down her window. She looked them over. "Are you all right?" she asked nervously.

Nancy glanced at her friends. They were a sorry sight. "We had a little accident," Nancy explained.

"I'm afraid we don't have room for you," the woman said. "But we'll stop at the nearest phone and call the police."

"Thanks."

Nancy watched them drive off.

"Think they'll really do it?" Ned asked.

"I hope so," Nancy said.

They had barely traveled half a mile when a state patrolman picked them up. He took them to the nearest police station, where they told the story of their kidnapping.

"We'll put out an APB for Slesak and Colville right away," one of the officers assured them.

"Is there any way we can get back to our hotel today?" Bess asked hopefully.

He smiled. "Arrangements are already being made."

They barely had time to offer their thanks before another officer drove them back to the Westerly. Exhaustion overtook them as soon as they entered the hotel and returned to their rooms to tumble into bed. *It's Sunday,* Nancy thought as she laid her head on her pillow. *Sunday, July twenty-ninth. Now why does that seem important?*

She was asleep before she could come up with the answer.

Someone was knocking on her door. Then her door unlatched. "Oh, pardon me. It's room service. You don't have your Do Not Disturb sign out." The door closed again.

Then Nancy awoke with a start. "July twenty-ninth!" she said. She tossed off her blankets and glanced at the clock. It was after noon. "Oh, no!" She banged her fist on the connecting door to George and Bess's room. "Wake up! Wake up!" she called. "Hurry! I've thought of something!"

A very tousled Bess pulled open the door. "This had better be good," she mumbled.

"The recipe," Nancy said. "Do you remember the proportions on the chocolate cake recipe? The one we talked about? Right at the top there were twenty-nine pounds of salt, and only seven of sugar."

"Am I dull, or what? I don't get it," Bess said with a yawn.

"Today's July twenty-ninth. It's the seventh month and the twenty-ninth day. It must have something to do with today's date!"

Bess rubbed her eyes. "So what's going on today?"

"I don't know. But I intend to find out. I'm going to try to reach Jacques Bonet. This time I'm going to ask him straight out what his involvement is."

She phoned Jacques's hotel room, but there was no answer. She called directory assistance for Claude DuPres's home number and was lucky enough to get it. She dialed the number and was surprised when the chef answered on the second ring.

"Hello," he said. "Claude DuPres speaking."

"Chef DuPres, it's Nancy Drew. I—uh, I was really trying to get hold of Jacques Bonet. I need to talk to him as soon as possible."

"Oh? Well, I'm afraid you will have to wait a few days. Jacques is out of town."

Nancy's heart sank. "Out of town? Do you know where?"

"He is in Washington, D.C. He left yesterday."

"The Washington dinner!" Nancy gasped. "Of course!" Suddenly it all made sense. All along Chef DuPres and Jacques Bonet had talked about this important dinner. She'd even wanted to know more about it herself. But what was going to happen there?

"Ms. Drew?" Chef DuPres asked. "Are you there?"

"Yes, Chef DuPres. Please, I don't have time to say more. I've got to contact Jacques."

"Ms. Drew! Please—a moment. Does this have anything to do with the threats against my life?"

Nancy was anxious to get off the phone. "I think so. But I won't know for certain until I talk to Jacques."

"Wait a moment. I will give you the address of the hotel where the dinner is taking place.

Jacques should be there." Chef DuPres told her the street address of a hotel in Georgetown, a prestigious section of Washington, D.C.

Something else clicked in Nancy's mind. As soon as she was off the phone, she wrote down as much as she could recall of that first recipe. She couldn't remember the rest of the proportions, but she did remember the preparation and cooking times—and they corresponded to the street address of the hotel!

Nancy's hand was shaking slightly as she dialed Jacques's hotel in Washington. "Carlisle Hotel," a woman answered.

"Please connect me with Jacques Bonet's room," Nancy said.

"One moment."

The line rang on and on. "I'm sorry," the desk clerk said, coming back on the line. "Mr. Bonet isn't in. Would you like to leave a message?"

"No. Thanks anyway."

There was only one thing left to do—go to Georgetown herself! Picking up the phone again, she dialed Ned's room. "Wake up, sleepyhead," she told him. "We've got some traveling to do."

"I'm awake and dressed, I'll have you know. What traveling?"

"I'll let you know at breakfast. The coffee shop in five minutes?"

"I'll be there."

Ned was waiting for her when she arrived. "So what's up?" he asked as they were shown to their table.

Nancy leaned forward on her elbows. "Today is July twenty-ninth. This is the date of the Washington dinner, the one where Jacques Bonet is taking Chef DuPres's place. Remember the chocolate cake recipe? The one we looked at in your room? The top two proportions were seven and twenty-nine?"

"The date of the dinner," Ned said and whistled.

"And that's not all. The address of the dinner corresponds to the preparation and cooking times."

"So where are we traveling?"

"To Washington, D.C. If my hunch is right, Jacques Bonet is right in the thick of things—whether he knows it or not!"

"What time is this dinner?" Ned asked.

"Claude said it's scheduled for seven-thirty. Ned, some very important international heads of state are going to be there. We won't be able to get in!"

"Call your father," Ned suggested. "We're going to need his help."

It took only a few phone calls for Carson Drew to contact Senator Kilpatrick, one of his personal friends, and pave the way for Nancy and Ned.

"Be careful," Carson told his only daughter.

"Always, Dad."

As Nancy tossed a few items in her purse, she brought Bess and George up to date on what was happening. "So I need you two to drive us to the airport," she finished. "Then come back and tell the local police about what's happening with Slesak and Colville. I'm sure they're both on their way to Washington."

"Don't worry, we'll take care of it. We just need to get you to the airport in time," said George.

George pushed the speed limit all the way to the airport. As they entered the terminal they heard their flight being called.

"Can we still get on the flight that's just leaving for Washington?" Nancy asked the ticket agent anxiously.

The agent punched up her records on the computer. "There are a few seats left," she said.

In record time the ticket agent collected their money and pointed them toward the gate. Nancy and Ned buckled in just as the plane started taxiing.

The airplane's tires touched down in Washington just as Ned's watch flicked to six-thirty. With rush-hour crowds it seemed to take forever for a taxi to arrive, but at last a bright yellow cab pulled up in front of them. "Where to?" the cabbie asked.

Nancy gave him the address of the hotel.

The cabbie drove to the outside gates of a

stately gray stone hotel. The entrance was cordoned off by ropes—and secret service men were everywhere.

Nancy walked up to the front door. "My name's Nancy Drew," she said, showing her identification to the first agent she encountered. "Senator Kilpatrick was going to call and— "

"It's all right, Ms. Drew. Both of you come along with me," he said. "Senator Kilpatrick relayed your message. You're to go straight inside. I'll take you."

"Thank you," Nancy said with relief.

They entered the main door of the hotel. Beyond the guards were rooms full of people —some of them very famous. "May we see the head chef, Jacques Bonet?" she asked their escort. "He's the reason we're here."

"I know," the agent said. "We've already been alerted about Slesak and Colville." He led them quickly to the back of the hotel.

The kitchen was huge and modern, with stainless steel counters, tiled walls, and what looked like hundreds of workers. Nancy glanced around anxiously, trying to pick Jacques out from the sea of white-coated chefs.

"Nancy!"

She spun around. Jacques was blinking at her in astonishment.

"What are *you* doing here?" he asked.

"Jacques, we need to talk to you. Privately."

He looked from Nancy to Ned, then back again. "What is it?"

"Paul Slesak and a cohort of his, someone named Colville, kidnapped us last night and tried to drown us in a lake."

"What?"

"They're involved in something big —something that has to do with this dinner. I'd say they're transferring political secrets, wouldn't you?"

Jacques glanced around, then pulled her and Ned to the side of the room, away from listening ears. "Why should I know?"

"Because you stole Slesak's recipes from him," Ned put in, watching Bonet's face closely. "You obviously knew something was going on."

Nancy held her breath. For a moment she didn't think Jacques was going to confide in them. Then he smiled crookedly and muttered, "So you found me out. Guess I'm not as clever as I thought I was."

"How are you involved?" Nancy asked.

He lifted his palms. "The truth is, I already knew about Slesak and Colville and their attempt to kidnap you."

"How?" Nancy asked.

"You reported it to the police, and they reported to federal agents. It was only a matter of time until they reported to me." He clasped Nancy's hand in his. "Congratulations.

You, Nancy Drew, have learned my secret."

"Which is?" she asked a trifle dazedly.

"That I'm working undercover with federal agents to crack open a ring of spies selling international secrets to the highest bidder. I'm not just a chef. I'm also a CIA agent!"

Chapter Seventeen

NANCY'S MOUTH DROPPED open. "You're an undercover agent for our government?"

Jacques inclined his head. "An intelligence agent."

"So you were on to Slesak all along?"

"I had my suspicions."

Jacques glanced around the kitchen again, then led Nancy and Ned toward another door. "I might as well tell you everything," he said. "Slesak has networks of people working for him. Informants in every country. Some of the people at this dinner tonight are more interested in gathering information against their enemies than in promoting peace. You can bet Slesak and Colville will show up here. They've got information to sell."

"So that's what the recipes are all about," Nancy said.

Jacques nodded. "The proportions and ingredients list important dates and places—for instance, this dinner. But we believe the code also reveals specific information concerning one country or another. In the wrong hands it could be lethal."

"Military information?" Nancy guessed.

"Among other things. Our government is working on cracking the trickier parts of the code." Jacques smiled wryly. "I stole the information from Slesak and pretended to be a buyer who wasn't interested in paying. I wanted to flush him out. But it backfired, and he turned on you.

"Thank you both for bringing me this information—but believe me, we were already primed and waiting for Slesak to show."

"You don't expect us to just leave, do you?" Nancy asked.

"Yes, I do."

"So which are you really?" Ned asked, as Jacques pushed them toward the door. "A chef, or a spy?"

"A little of both." Jacques's smile was almost cruel. "I like excitement. Being a chef isn't quite enough of a challenge."

They had almost reached the side entrance when several men hurried to Jacques's side. "An unscheduled delivery van is outside," one said quietly. "But it's empty."

"Slesak." Nancy breathed out loud. "He's loose."

Jacques's face grew dark with annoyance. "Get them out of here," he commanded, jerking his head at Nancy and Ned.

"We can't. We've blocked the entrances," another man said.

"Stay here. I'll be right back."

Nancy hovered near the corner, watching as Jacques strode off after the two men. She was secretly delighted. "Slesak can't get inside past this security," she said.

"I wouldn't think so," Ned said.

After a few moments Nancy said, "What do you think's going on out there?"

"I don't know, but I'll go look," Ned said.

"I'm coming with you."

"One of us should stay here in case Jacques comes back." Ned sounded as if his mind were made up.

Nancy stood and watched him go. She felt uneasy all by herself. She decided to check out what was on the other side of the kitchen. She pushed open the swinging door—and was immediately accosted by a bevy of federal agents. "Get her out of here!" one of them yelled, and Nancy was shoved into another room.

Nancy turned around and was amazed to see that she was in the ballroom. "I wish Ned were with me," she said, hearing her voice echo hollowly back at her.

Nancy paced the floor, growing more and more restless. She was starting up a central marble staircase that led to a balcony when the main door suddenly swung inward and Jacques appeared.

"I thought I told you to stay where you were! Where's Ned?"

"Looking for you," Nancy told him, coming back down the stairs. "Listen, we might have some information that could help. I heard Colville say something about a double cross. Do you think he's planning to sell fake documents to someone?"

Jacques seemed to be thinking hard. "All I know is that Colville was Slesak's contact on this job," he said after a minute. "We don't know who's buying the information, but as soon as we nab Colville and Slesak, it won't matter anyhow."

"You've been tracking Slesak a long time, haven't you?"

"For years. Slesak has used his cover as a chef to get himself on the staff of many important political dinners. And not just in this country.

When he settled at Claude's school, I began to wonder what was going on. Then I realized that he needed the school's reputation because he was losing his own."

"The night you came to Slesak's office—"

"I was trying to steal the recipes then," Jacques admitted. "I'd gone through them once before, but Slesak had interrupted me. Then the second time I went back, you were there." He smiled. "Your friend's wallet was an excuse, wasn't it?"

Nancy nodded. "I wanted to know why Slesak was so worried about those recipes too. Sorry I didn't trust you then."

"No problem. I didn't trust you either. Any more questions?"

"What about Trent Richards?"

"Richards!" Jacques shook his head. "A two-bit blackmailer who got in over his head. Slesak got tired of his demands, knocked him out, and left him in the freezer. He made sure the lock on the door was broken."

"What about the accidents?"

"They were simply designed to get rid of Claude. Slesak knew he could blame Claude for lax security and get the board on his side. Eventually he could be head of the school."

"So the wrought-iron rack could have fallen at any time? That's funny. I had the strangest feeling it was meant for me."

Jacques hesitated. "Maybe it was. Slesak could

have been waiting for you to come to the front of the room."

Nancy nodded. It all made perfect sense. Her instincts about Paul Slesak had been right from the beginning.

Jacques examined his watch, then listened at the door. "Maybe we should find out what's going on," Nancy suggested. She was starting to get worried about Ned.

"No. I'm keeping my eye on you. I don't want you involved."

"But Ned's already out there."

"He'll have to take care of himself."

Nancy rubbed her palms together nervously. "What time is it now?" she asked.

Jacques flicked a glance at his watch. "Seven-thirty," he said flatly.

But Nancy hardly heard him. Her eyes were glued to his wrist, where a semicircle of toothprints showed. *Her* toothprints.

Nancy's pulse started beating in her temples. She had bitten her white-robed assailant's wrist the other night. It had been Jacques Bonet's wrist! He was the man who had attacked her!

Nancy edged away from him. Sweat was breaking out on her forehead. Jacques was a *double* agent. He had tried to kill her once before. He would undoubtedly try again.

Now she understood what Colville's reference to double-crossing meant. Now she knew why Jacques had her alone with him.

Nancy backed away until she stood in the center of the room. On the balcony above she could see several doors. Any one of them might lead to freedom.

She sidled closer to the stairway. What would Jacques do if she just turned and ran? Attack her again? She remembered how strong he was. She could never win a battle with him.

But she had to escape.

"Stay back," Jacques said. Nancy froze, sure she'd been found out. But he was just opening the door, checking outside.

This was her chance!

Nancy dashed up the stairs as fast as she could, her heart pounding. The first landing was only about a dozen steps up.

"What the—?" Jacques asked, spinning around.

Nancy kept on running. Her breath came in gasps. She was almost there!

Then a loud bang suddenly went off behind her—and the stairway rail exploded beside her head.

"Better stop running, Ms. Drew," Jacques said coldly. "Or the next bullet's for you."

Chapter Eighteen

NANCY STOOD FROZEN in place, staring down at Bonet. How had she ever thought he was handsome? There was nothing remotely attractive about the hardened criminal in front of her.

"You were just a little too smart, weren't you?" he asked, aiming his gun at her head.

"You can't get away now," Nancy said, her voice calm. "Federal agents are all over the place."

"Federal agents who trust me. And you're not going to betray me, if you want to keep on living."

Keep him talking, Nancy thought. It's the only way.

"So Slesak isn't the only one selling international secrets," she said softly. "You're working for him."

"You've got that backward. He was working for me—until he decided to take matters into his own hands. Paul's problem is that he's greedy. He isn't willing to wait."

"And the accidents at the school? Those were Slesak's doing?"

Jacques snorted in disgust. "The imbecile! He wanted that school so badly he was willing to risk our entire operation. He tried to run Claude down, and when that didn't work, he poisoned him. Then he went to the papers!"

"What about Claude? Where does he fit in?"

"He's only a foolish old man." Jacques's gun hand was steady. Too steady for Nancy to risk another escape.

"So you used him. You earned your own reputation by hanging onto his coattails."

"I am an excellent chef," Jacques said coolly. "I'm an even better agent. Now, enough questions. You and I are going for a ride."

Before Nancy could move, the doors to the room suddenly burst open and Ned came flying toward Jacques—unarmed.

Nancy screamed.

Jacques turned. His gun was pointed straight at Ned's head.

Nancy threw herself at Jacques. The gun went off and flew out of Jacques's hand, skittering across the polished floor.

Nancy held on to Jacques with all her strength. But it was only a matter of seconds before he had freed himself, throwing her aside like a rag doll.

Then Ned was on top of him.

Instantly the room was crowded with secret service agents. Nancy jumped to her feet.

Ned and Jacques were still rolling across the floor. Finally Ned got a choke hold on Jacques. "Bonet," he said through clenched teeth, "it's all over now."

Four hours later, after a long session with federal agents, Nancy and Ned were released.

Within an hour they were waiting by their assigned gate for their flight home.

"You really want to finish our cooking lessons, huh?" Nancy asked Ned. "After all this excitement, don't you think cooking school is going to be a letdown?"

"Are you kidding? I'll welcome the change!"

Nancy smiled. "I'm glad all Slesak's recipe cards were turned in. Now maybe the government can decode all the information," she said.

"They should ask you to help them. You figured out the date of the Washington dinner."

"The easy part," she said, smiling. "I don't think even Jacques knew everything in those files."

"Jacques was clever though," Ned said after a moment. "He almost had me convinced that he was on the level until I heard that shot go off in the ballroom."

"He had me fooled," said Nancy, glancing out the window at an approaching plane. "But I don't know who was worse, Bonet or Slesak. Slesak tried to kill me with the wrought-iron holder. He was the one waiting in the vent above."

"Yeah, but who got you to the front of the room? Bonet." Ned's mouth tightened. "And Bonet was the one who tackled you on the street.

"Bonet is definitely the true villain here," Ned continued. "He ordered Slesak to fool with the stove and try either to kill Richards or scare him off. And he was the one who masterminded Richards's death."

"Because Richards was blackmailing him. It was *Jacques* I heard being threatened in the hallway that night," Nancy said with a sigh. Hearing the announcement that their plane was ready for boarding, they started walking to the gate. "But Colville was the one who fooled with the elevator, and that was on Slesak's orders. Bonet was trying hard to hold down the publicity. Especially after Slesak went to the press."

"Are you defending Bonet?" Ned asked curiously.

"Good grief, no! The point is, he and Slesak are two of a kind. Both interested in achieving what they want, whatever the cost." Nancy handed the flight attendant her boarding pass and made her way to her seat. "It's all pretty hard to believe, isn't it?" she said as Ned settled down beside her. "But I guess now we know why Bonet paid me so much attention. He wanted to keep an eye on me at all times."

"If you say so." Ned pulled a magazine out of the seat pocket in front of him. "Personally, I think he's just attracted to danger. And you're a dangerous, beautiful, intelligent detective."

"Oh?"

"Yeah. And you know, I have learned a few things at cooking school. And one of them is that cooking is like chess. It just takes a little practice."

"I've heard chess is boring," Nancy said with a smile.

"Oh, yeah? Those people haven't had me to teach them."

Nancy glanced sideways at him. Ned's eyes glinted with humor. "Okay, I'll bite. What's so great about the way you teach chess?"

"Well, for someone such as yourself, it's going to take hours and hours of practice."

"Meaning what?"

"Meaning, we'll have to spend a lot of time together—just you and me—practicing." A smile threatened the corners of his mouth.

"Practicing—moves?" Nancy asked innocently.

"Yeah." He grinned. "I think you're catching on."

"These moves. Could you give me an example of one?"

For an answer he leaned forward, kissing her in a way that made her heart beat a bit faster. "That's an opening move," he said.

"I see." Nancy took a deep breath. "Well, I may need a lot of lessons."

"Practice makes perfect." Ned grinned, then kissed her again.

As the plane began roaring up the runway, Nancy said softly, "I think I'm going to like chess."

And they both laughed.

Nancy's next case:

Nancy finds herself in a delicate situation when newspaper publisher Frazier Carlton asks her to check out his daughter Brenda's latest boyfriend —and keep the investigation a secret. When Brenda sees Nancy talking to Mike McKeever, she assumes that Nancy's interest is personal, not professional. Still worse, Mike is attracted to Nancy. Now Ned isn't happy.

But Mr. Carlton is right to worry: Brenda may have taken up with a fortune hunter. As Nancy traces Mike's past, she learns that Mike has had other rich girlfriends and that one of them turned up missing. Now Nancy is concerned that more than Brenda's affections is in danger. Even if she gets to Brenda in time, will Brenda thank Nancy for breaking up her romance? Find out in FATAL ATTRACTION, Case #22 in The Nancy Drew Files™.

HAVE YOU SEEN THE HARDY BOYS® LATELY?

Bond has high-tech equipment, Indiana Jones courage and daring...

ONLY THE HARDY BOYS CASE FILES HAVE IT ALL!!

THE HARDY BOYS
CASE FILES

- **#1 DEAD ON TARGET** 62558/$2.50
- **#2 EVIL, INC.** 62559/$2.50
- **#3 CULT OF CRIME** 62128/$2.50
- **#4 THE LAZARUS PLOT** 62129/$2.75
- **#5 EDGE OF DESTRUCTION** 62646/$2.75
- **#6 THE CROWNING TERROR** 62647/$2.75
- **#7 DEATHGAME** 62648/$2.75
- **#8 SEE NO EVIL** 62649/$2.75
- **#9 THE GENIUS THIEVES** 63080/$2.75
- **#10 HOSTAGES OF HATE** 63081/$2.75
- **#11 BROTHER AGAINST BROTHER** 63082/$2.75
- **#12 PERFECT GETAWAY** 63083/$2.75
- **#13 THE BORGIA DAGGER** 64463/$2.75

Simon & Schuster, Mail Order Dept. ASD
200 Old Tappan Rd., Old Tappan, N.J. 07675

Please send me the books I have checked above. I am enclosing $________ (please add 75¢ to cover postage and handling for each order. N.Y.S. and N.Y.C. residents please add appropriate sales tax). Send check or money order–no cash or C.O.D.'s please. Allow up to six weeks for delivery. For purchases over $10.00 you may use VISA: card number, expiration date and customer signature must be included.

Name ____

Address ____

City ______________________ State/Zip ______________

VISA Card No. ______________________ Exp. Date ______________

Signature ____ 120-01